# Look for these titles by
# *Bonnie Dee*

## *Now Available:*

Finding Home (with Lauren Baker)
Evolving Man
Blackberry Pie
Opposites Attract
Perfecting Amanda
The Valentine Effect
The Countess Takes a Lover
The Final Act
Empath
The Countess Lends a Hand
Butterfly Unpinned (with Laura Bacchi)
The Thief and the Desert Flower
Star Flyer

*Fairytale Fantasies*
(with Marie Treanor)
Cinderella Unmasked
Demon Lover
Awakening Beauty
Sex and the Single Princess

*Magical Menages*
Shifters' Captive
Vampires' Consort

*Print Anthologies*
Heat Wave
Strangers in the Night
Gifted

Look for these titles by
*Summer Devon*

*Now Available:*

Learning Charity
Revealing Skills
The Knight's Challenge
Taken Unaware
Unnatural Calamities

*Print Anthology*
I Dream of Dragons, Volume 1

# The Psychic and the Sleuth

*Bonnie Dee and Summer Devon*

Samhain Publishing, Ltd.
11821 Mason Montgomery Road, 4B
Cincinnati, OH 45249
www.samhainpublishing.com

The Psychic and the Sleuth
Copyright © 2012 by Bonnie Dee and Summer Devon
Print ISBN: 978-1-60928-843-3
Digital ISBN: 978-1-60928-697-2

Editing by Linda Ingmanson
Cover by Kendra Egert

This book is a work of fiction. The names, characters, places, and incidents are products of the writer's imagination or have been used fictitiously and are not to be construed as real. Any resemblance to persons, living or dead, actual events, locale or organizations is entirely coincidental.

All Rights Are Reserved. No part of this book may be used or reproduced in any manner whatsoever without written permission, except in the case of brief quotations embodied in critical articles and reviews.

First Samhain Publishing, Ltd. electronic publication: January 2012
First Samhain Publishing, Ltd. print publication: December 2012

# Dedication

To all our loyal readers who've enjoyed our historicals. Hope you enjoy this paranormal mystery which once again brings together two opposites with a powerful attraction to each other.

# Chapter One

*London, 1892*

"I'm getting a name. I believe it starts with a W." The young man in the checked jacket spoke in the sepulchral tone one expected from a Spiritualistic medium. Lush, dark lashes fluttered against his cheeks, and full lips parted as his eyebrows drew together in a frown.

He might sound the part, but his appearance was wrong, Court decided. His clothes, for one thing. Most mediums he'd observed wore dark, dignified clothing, as if to lend gravity to their incredible claims. Oliver Marsh's scarlet waistcoat and checked jacket were too flashy by far for the role he was playing. Made him appear more like a fly-by-night salesman than a portal to the other world.

"Wilma? No. Winifred." Marsh's head cocked as though hearing an unseen voice whisper the name in his ear.

Court forced his eyes not to roll at the act. The young lady beside him gasped, and her limp, clammy hand gripped his tighter. "I have an aunt named Winifred. She died two years ago."

The spiritualist inclined his head. "I'm getting the sense of her presence, a sense of great love and peace. She's content on the other side, but she has a message she needs to deliver."

Miss Abigail Fontaine leaned forward, eyes wide. "What does she want to tell me?"

Mr. Marsh's frown deepened, and he moved his head slowly from side to side as though searching for a sound that came in intermittent bursts. "She says..." A long pause. "Don't. There is something you are about to do, a big decision. She's warning you against making the wrong choice."

The redhead gasped again, and her grip on Court's hand became almost painful. "Rodney? Aunt Winifred doesn't approve of my fiancé, Mr. Pepperidge? But that's impossible. Why not? Ask her why not?"

Court's jaw tightened as he watched the medium play the young woman like an angler taking his time reeling in a fish. He didn't know how Marsh had secured the details of the Fontaine woman's engagement or why he would interfere. Perhaps her family or the Pepperidges didn't approve the match and had paid Marsh to encourage Miss Fontaine to end it. Any scenario was feasible except for the possibility that Miss Fontaine's aunt was actually transmitting a message from beyond the grave.

It was Court's job to expose Marsh as a charlatan to stop him from taking money from gullible people. Posing as a believer, he'd observe the man until he was able to prove he'd fleeced a customer or coerced money from someone. Because he'd been too damned persistent on a case that hadn't been assigned to him, Court no longer hunted murderers. It was some consolation to reflect that he would be stopping a predator. A man who gave false hope to the desperate was the lowest sort of scum.

He would maintain his cover so he could continue to interact with the spiritualist. Soon enough the false medium would be arrested, ending another shameful career.

Marsh paused and frowned some more, belaboring the effort it took to reach through the mists of time and space to reach the dead. "This spirit seems to feel your young man is not all he has represented himself to be. I'm getting two messages from her, a sense of deep love for you and a clear warning, but nothing more specific."

Court had tracked another medium a few years earlier—that one had stolen works of art during weekend parties—and he'd been to enough séances now to know the routine. At this point, the medium usually snapped out of his or her trance, making a great show of weariness, and would leave the table. The excited guests would break for refreshments as they pondered his great spiritual gift and discussed the messages. In Court's opinion, there was more thrill-seeking than actual spiritual resonance about these affairs.

But tonight the medium didn't immediately open those long-lashed eyes. Instead, he held very still, and his face turned markedly pale. He caught his breath before he spoke again, and when he did, his voice was low and rasping, scraping up Court's spine like a file. "There is another presence."

Their hostess and fervent spiritualist, Lady Markham, was beside herself with excitement at the prospect of more messages from beyond. "Are you all right, Mr. Marsh?"

"Oh God." Marsh grimaced as though in pain. "She is... She needs..." he stammered.

"Who? Do you have a name?" Lady Markham murmured, anxious not to break the medium's concentration at this delicate moment.

"A flower. White. Not a daisy. She's"—Marsh caught his breath and exhaled a name—"Lily."

Court felt like someone had driven a fist into his stomach. Lily. The image of his cousin's face came to him. God, he wished he could see a picture of Lily laughing, but no, he saw the moment of her death. Every detail from the blood oozing from the back of her head, to the anguish in her eyes just before they closed for the last time—he bit down on the inside of his cheek to stop himself seeing the rest. God damn Marsh.

"The man scared her. He said she'll join the others." Marsh's voice was anguished and his expression contorted. It was quite a performance, and Court was having a hard time keeping his dyspeptic stomach from lurching. The medium must know he was a police inspector and his true purpose in attending the séance. But how had Marsh found out about Lily?

Marsh choked on a sob. "She's looking at Robert."

"Robert Littleton?" Lady Markham looked at the white-haired gentleman seated across the table from her.

"Not I, madam." Littleton's handlebar moustache twitched as he spoke. "There's never been a woman named Lily in my life."

Robert Court stirred uneasily. He hadn't given his first name when he'd contacted Lady Markham about her interesting new protégé; he'd simply called himself Mr. Peeler, the name he often used for this sort of work.

What was Marsh's goal? What did he hope to achieve by baiting him? Court wanted to let go of the sweaty palm of the man named Abernathy on his left and Miss Fontaine's slender hand on his right to jump up and walk away from the table, but he mustn't react to Marsh's words. He couldn't let any of them know who he truly was, and they *would* interrogate him if they thought the pronouncement from beyond held meaning for him.

"He said there were others," the medium's desolate voice continued. "Murder. Murder."

"Oh my goodness." The elderly woman beside Miss Fontaine broke the circle and reached for her handkerchief to dab at her forehead. "This is too much, Lady Markham. Entirely too much. I don't wish to participate any longer."

"Shh, Marjorie," their hostess said. "A murderer's identity

may be revealed here tonight. What greater purpose could there be for these gatherings than to bring about truth and justice?" Diamonds flashed in Lady Markham's ears, matching the sparkle in her eyes. Her ladyship was the type of woman who wore jewels even for an informal gathering with friends, overdressed and with too much time on her idle hands, but a caring person at heart, Court believed. She'd be appalled to learn she was the reason her good friend Mr. Marsh had come under the gaze of the authorities.

The relatively minor case of a spiritual medium had been handed to the serious-crimes officer because Marsh had begun to bilk the wealthy. Lord Markham disliked having his wife throw money at Marsh and had complained to Sir Bradford, the commissioner.

"Carry on, Mr. Marsh," Lady Markham said. "What else does Lily say?"

Court studied the medium's face, noting how his eyes darted back and forth beneath the lids. He was quite an actor, with a full arsenal of emotions in his quiver. Tears leaked from the corners of his closed eyes and rolled down his cheeks. Court watched in fascination as they dripped off that smooth-shaven jaw onto his crisp white shirt collar and felt a ridiculous urge to lean forward and wipe away the tears.

*It's all a sham*, he reminded himself. *Bits of facts stitched together with fancy.* A swindler was adept at learning everything about the people he planned to cheat and then striking them at their Achilles' heel. How Marsh had learned about the Lily Bailey case was all that mattered.

"He was stronger than I imagined. I didn't listen to you about being careful, dear. I should have listened to you. Oh, Phillip," Marsh whispered the words.

Court felt another blow to his gut, for only he had heard

those words after he'd been summoned to the scene by the constable. She'd returned to consciousness for a few heartbeats, whispered the few garbled phrases, just as roughly as Marsh had, and no one else had been within hearing distance. Another thought came to him—there might be a simple explanation why Marsh might have been lurking so close. He could be the murderer. Court swallowed his nausea.

"Weak. Tired. Dizzy." What the hell did that mean? For a moment, Court felt excitement that Lily was saying something new. Idiotic.

*False hope for the desperate.*

After delivering the cryptic message, Marsh gave a strangled groan and slumped forward. His head dropped to his chest as if he were a marionette with cut strings. Court knew the routine. In a moment, he'd lift his head and blink, pretending to come out of a trance.

As Lady Markham's guests released each other's hands and murmured together about what they'd witnessed, the medium did not regain consciousness. In fact, he leaned precariously to the left in the armless chair and began to fall. Court leaped from his own seat two places away and caught the man's body as it tumbled from the chair. His muscles were lax as if he truly were unconscious. Court lowered the body to the floor while the other guests gathered around, chattering like excited children.

He must dig deeper, for he had a charlatan and now possible murderer to deal with, carefully. Court would lose his position entirely if he kept insisting Childs had nabbed the wrong man in the case of Lily Bailey's murder. From the start, Superintendent Hardy had made it clear Court had no right to interfere in the case, but that hadn't stopped Court's private investigation. It only made him more careful.

And damnation, if he found the real killer—*when* he did—

he'd hand the evidence to that lazy bastard Childs. That would ensure the case against the real murderer would hold up. Of course, he might take a less official route once he discovered Lily's killer.

He straightened and considered how he'd go about finding the truth regarding the young man lying at his feet.

Lady Markham went to find her smelling salts, and Miss Fontaine fanned the medium's pale face with a pamphlet she'd snatched from a side table. The cover read *Reaching Out to the Other Side*. Court loosened Marsh's tie and unfastened his shirt collar. He was uncomfortably aware of the weight of the man's shoulders settling against his arm and of the tiny movement of Marsh's pulse throbbing in his bared throat. Court despised himself for his attraction to the handsome man, not because such feelings were a perversion. At the very least, Marsh was a scoundrel, an enemy of the people, and it was Court's duty to stop his ruthless deception of innocent people.

And yet, it appeared the man really *had* fainted, though he might be resorting to adept trickery. But to what purpose? Unless this little show was specifically to put Court off guard and make him doubt his skepticism. Or he was a murderer hoping to be caught.

As he bent over the medium, Court inhaled a whiff of spicy cologne emanating from his warm skin and mingling with clean sweat. Marsh's lips were plump and full with a bow in the upper lip. A lock had loosened from the pomade slicking his hair back and lay against his forehead. More brown curls threatened to break free, and suddenly Court wanted to see that hair with no pomade, just a riot of curls in revolt.

He ignored the heat gathering in his groin and gave Marsh a smart slap across the jaw to wake him up. Perhaps he put a little too much strength behind the slap. As Lady Markham rushed up with a small flask of smelling salts, Marsh's impossibly long eyelashes flickered, and his eyes opened and focused on Court's face. Their vivid blue gave them an unearthly, far-seeing appearance. The gullible might easily believe a man with such unusual eyes could see into the ethereal realm. But Court knew better.

He lowered Marsh's upper body to the floor and sat back on his heels. "Are you all right, Mr. Marsh?"

"Yes, thank you. I'm not sure what came over me." His voice was low and breathless. He struggled to sit, and Court took his hand to pull him up. Marsh's hand was warm and firm, and the sandalwood scent of India floated around him like the spirits he claimed surrounded people at all times. Court pulled him up hard, but Marsh didn't stumble as he gained his feet. He was stronger than his slight figure appeared.

"I'm sorry," Marsh apologized to their hostess. "Nothing like this has happened to me before."

"It's no wonder. You must have been overcome by the strength of Lily's emotions," her ladyship replied. Court flinched at the sound of the name.

"A murdered girl. Imagine!" the elderly woman chimed in.

"How much do you recall of what is said by the spirits you host? Are you aware throughout the trance?" John Littleton asked.

Court's estimation of the older man rose. It was a logical question. He was curious how Marsh would answer.

"Yes, I'm aware, Mr. Littleton. Being a channel is a bit like standing on one side of a gauze curtain and watching a play through that filter. I'm conscious of everyone in the room, including my own body, but I'm divorced from the physical." He was fluent and wore a half smile again. "I can hear the spirits clamoring to be heard, more as thoughts than actual voices.

Sometimes I even see a hint of their ethereal forms."

Still slightly nauseated, Court searched the man's face for the telltale signs of a liar. A hand to his face. Eyes held too still or eyes that shifted too often signified he was prevaricating. But Mr. Marsh spoke without a twitch. Maybe he'd deluded himself that he was hearing voices. A mania of the mind perhaps.

Marsh started to climb to his feet, and again Court found himself supporting him. He grasped the other man's arm and held it until Marsh was steady on his feet.

Eyes the color of periwinkles met his. "Thank you, Mr. Peeler."

He dipped his head in acknowledgment and adopted the tone of an earnest devotee. "You've done us all a great honor by allowing us a glimpse through that mystic veil, Mr. Marsh. Thank *you*."

Marsh's brows knitted slightly as if he heard sarcasm in Court's tone.

The ladies took over after that, brushing past Court to surround Mr. Marsh and coo over him as ladies were wont to do.

"Come sit on the chaise," Lady Markham urged.

"Perhaps a glass of sherry?" Mrs. Banning suggested.

Miss Fontaine offered her handkerchief dampened in a water glass to press against Marsh's forehead. "Do you know anything more about why my dear departed aunt doesn't approve my fiancé? What has he done?"

Marsh blinked slowly. "Miss Fontaine, the communications I receive from beyond are often very vague, more like strong impressions than detailed messages. I couldn't say."

Court almost admired how these mediums had a ready answer for any question. They were as slippery as politicians and equally as likely to lie through their teeth. But the money they received for their services was always freely given, not solicited as a payment; thus it was difficult to stop their game. Working vice cases was in some ways more difficult than homicide, where at least the crime was cut and dried. The unfortunate choice of words brought to his mind memories of the sliced body parts he'd encountered on his last homicide case—the one before Lily. He stared at Oliver Marsh, whom the ladies had sat on a chaise longue and were supplying with brandy. *What is your game, Mr. Marsh? Beware of playing against me.*

Oliver felt like he'd been hit with a twenty-pound sledgehammer, and sitting in an airless parlor with perfume-drenched biddies crowding around him wasn't helping him recover. He needed to get outside, draw a deep lungful of fresh, coal-scented air, then have a couple of cigarettes and something stronger than the thimbleful of sherry he'd been given.

Jesus Christ, he was losing his damned mind. For a few moments, he'd lost track of himself as he heard a voice speaking and a presence intruding on his consciousness. He'd always explained to his clients that he observed the room and his body at a distance while tuning in to another world beyond the physical. Well, the real experience was somewhat different, as if his brain was full of static energy and he could see-hear-feel the thoughts and impressions of another being sharing his mind. Pure poppycock, his father would've said, but nevertheless, there it was. He'd had an honest-to-God psychic experience, and then he'd blacked out.

He glanced up and met the steady gaze of the sandy-haired fellow whose face had been hovering over his when he came to. Lady Markham had introduced him as Mr. Peeler. Oliver had felt the man's focus on him all evening, studying, weighing, assessing. Peeler was a skeptic. Oliver could spot one a mile away, and he usually knew just the right thing to say to lay their fears to rest and convince them he was legitimate. Half-truths and generalizations were a medium's best friend.

But tonight... Damn, he couldn't get that voice out of his head even now. Not really a voice, more of an inner thought, but a thought that wasn't his own. The definite female manifestation had been filled with sorrow, and he'd felt every bit of her mournful presence. Oliver considered himself a fairly optimistic person, but she'd left him as drippy as a sodden dishrag. Such pain, such a sense of fucking loss. God, he wished he could shut it out of his mind.

"I'm sorry, Lady Markham, but I must be going." He pushed off the chaise, scattering the ladies as he rose. "Thank you for inviting me tonight. I hope I've been of some help to your guests."

He held Miss Fontaine's gaze for a moment, hoping she'd take his message to heart. It had been delivered courtesy of the Pepperidge family, who did not wish their wayward son to marry beneath his station. Unfortunately, the man had already offered for the Fontaine girl sans their approval, and now it was up to them to end the relationship without incurring the scandal of a broken engagement. Knowing Abigail Fontaine's predilection for the occult, the family solicitor had contacted Oliver to help end the matter. A message from the other side could be a powerful deterrent to headstrong young love. But Oliver didn't much care if the ruse worked or not. He'd be paid for his services either way.

"Shall I have one of the butlers call a hansom cab for you, Mr. Marsh?" Lady Markham asked. "You seem shaky and hardly fit to walk. What do you think this spirit, Lily, is trying to say to us? What must we do for her?"

"I couldn't say, madam. I'm only the mouthpiece for restless souls. I can't decipher what their messages mean. Only the ones here on earth who have a relationship with them understand the meaning." Oliver was getting desperate to get out of the room. It was starting to feel like a nightmare in which he couldn't get his feet moving, and the lady was right, his legs were still trembling and his head spinning. It would be humiliating to faint again.

"We can share a cab. I'll see you home." Mr. Peeler was suddenly beside him again. For a moment, Oliver thought Peeler might take his arm, keep him standing upright. For a moment, he wanted him to, needed to feel that strong hand gripping his arm and supporting him. Foolish thought.

He straightened his shoulders and willed his jelly legs to stone. It would be better to get his own ride. Did he really want to be questioned by a skeptic all the way home? But on the other hand, maybe Mr. Peeler had some business proposition he wanted to discuss. Oliver was always looking for new clients, so it wouldn't hurt to hear what the man had to say.

"I'd appreciate that. Thank you," Oliver answered at last. "But I'm clear over near Northhampton Square. Is that too out of your way?"

"Not at all." The sandy-haired man seemed in almost as much of a hurry to leave as Oliver. He bid good-bye to the other guests, promising to attend the next scheduled event of their semi-secret society; then he strode toward the front hall, where a footman surrendered his hat, coat and umbrella.

Oliver felt like a leaf caught in a stream and carried along by the energy of the other man as he accepted his outerwear from the footman and followed Peeler to the street, where he hailed a hansom.

He climbed onto the seat inside the enclosed carriage, his

left knee bumping Peeler's right. It was only a graze, innocent, nothing, and yet Oliver felt a shiver of...something shoot through him. Anticipation? Lust? He glanced at Peeler, trying to read those gray eyes for the silent message that certain men gave other men. The communication was as ephemeral as the fake spirits Oliver conjured at his séances but very tangible—if it was the right sort of man.

But he couldn't quite read Peeler's eyes. The message was unclear. Perhaps he had not yet come to terms with his base desires—thus the struggle that Oliver thought he saw in the other man's gaze. At any rate, not knowing if Peeler was so inclined, he refrained from rubbing his knee against the other man's.

"Where are your lodgings?" Peeler asked, and after Oliver told him, he rapped on the slider and informed the driver.

"I hope I'm not putting you out of your way," Oliver repeated to fill the silence that followed. "Where do you live?"

"Not far, but I don't mind taking a detour."

It was a bit more than a detour, being clear across town, but Oliver wasn't going to press the point. He waited quietly for the bubble of silence to burst and Peeler's real reason for giving him a ride to come pouring out. He watched his traveling companion's face when it was lit by flashes of streetlamps.

Mr. Peeler had an angular, solid face that would've been at home on a boxer. Strong jaw, square chin, broad nose and a slight overhang of the brow. Oliver wondered about Peeler's background. There was some military in his past, that was easy to see from his stiff posture. Too bad Oliver hadn't known that before this session. Researching the guest list for one of his séances was an important part of his job, but he'd been able to find very little about Mr. Peeler. He hadn't even had time to pry his first name from Lady Markham.

"I understand you're in the import business. That must be very interesting," Oliver ventured.

Peeler stared at him, and in the dark, tight space, Oliver suddenly felt quite nervous and a great deal aroused. Something simmered in the air between them, a mixture of impending danger and breathless anticipation, as if they were poised on the brink of something astonishing. Like the odd experience earlier, Oliver had never felt anything quite like it.

"What?" he asked in response to a question that hadn't been asked aloud.

"I should be the one asking you 'what', Mr. Marsh." The low voice was almost a physical force caressing his skin and making him shiver. "What was all that about Lily? You *were* speaking of Lily Bailey, and we both know it."

Oliver gaped at him. So much for his ability at guessing a man's thoughts. He might not get messages from the next world, but he usually was sharp enough to pick up on the ones floating around this one.

He wasn't sure if the flash of heat he'd felt was mutual. But he would have bet three sittings' fees that Peeler was going to accuse him of being a cheat and liar. Instead, he was confronted by this Lily topic again.

Oliver nervously licked his lips. The other man's eyes narrowed, watching his mouth. So they shared that sort of appetite after all. He briefly wondered if Peeler even knew he showed signs of thwarted desire. So many men hid their craving even from themselves.

Oliver forced his breath to steady. There was something off about this fellow, a lie somewhere in there under that appealing, upright figure. He smacked of authority, but at least Oliver wasn't going to have to face that tiresome accusation of chicanery.

On the other hand, all this bleating about "Lily" meant nothing to Oliver, beyond the strange incident at Lady Markham's. Oliver had never had what his grandmother used to call "a strange turn". He was still rattled by the otherworldly experience and couldn't blithely shove it off and come up with a string of nonsense to explain his flash of whatever the hell that was to Peeler. Or to himself.

He wished he could smoke. That would settle his thoughts and allow him to figure out what the devil was going on. Peeler seemed to have some information about the origin of the odd episode. He hoped the other man might confirm that Oliver only had a moment of weakness. Yes. The whole thing had been so disturbing, he decided to say something that hinted at his methods.

"Perhaps I read something about Lily in a newspaper," he said. That would be good—combine an article he'd read with some passing illness, and he'd been babbling while half-conscious.

"No." Peeler's voice was low but firm. "The details you mentioned were never in the newspapers."

"No?" he said weakly, then was hit with a realization. Jesus God, maybe Peeler was the murderer and that was why Oliver sensed his air of a lie. It could explain why Peeler knew all about this Lily. Oliver slipped a hand into the pocket on the inside of his coat and felt for the slender, sheathed knife he carried for protection.

"I really couldn't tell you where I got the words," he said, speaking the truth at last. "I don't know any more about it than you do." Or so he prayed.

"Lily Bailey was murdered November fifth of last year. I knew her well. And I was there as she died. But I expect you know that already, don't you."

# Chapter Two

Court could've kicked himself for throwing the card of Lily's story on the table. Even as the words were coming out of his mouth, he didn't know why he was talking about Lily to the very man he was trying to expose. He was better at his job than this. He knew how to poke and prod and gather information until he'd woven a web from which his guilty victim couldn't escape. Then down came the full force of the law, eliminating the wrongdoer and ridding society of one more crawling insect.

"Look here." Marsh slid away from Court and pushed against the door of the carriage. "Mr. Peeler, what's your game? You're watching me like a spider watches a fly."

How odd that they should both think of Marsh as a bug. Court smiled at the coincidence. He liked the way Marsh flinched at his smile.

Perhaps it was best to let the man know he was under observation. Perhaps he'd make a stupid mistake. Court didn't have the authority to pursue the matter of Lily, but he would push as best he could in the other matter of fraud. He leaned forward, not above using a little physical intimidation to get honest answers from Marsh. "My game? You're the one who plays, Mr. Marsh. You go into your little sessions armed with information about your marks."

Marsh gazed at him, that disturbing mouth steady, his blue eyes revealing nothing. For a few moments, he'd been shaken, pale, truly upset about something. Guilty conscience, perhaps?

But now he'd managed to regain his equilibrium. He glared back at Court as if he was the aggrieved party. "I don't know what you mean, Mr. Peeler. Perhaps you should let me out."

To hell with Childs and the superintendent's threats. A sudden fury seized Court. He'd push Marsh over that edge of calm again and get a straight answer from him.

Court ignored him. "I think you're worse than a fraud. What you did back there, that little speech about Lily was more. You know it, and I do too. And I'm not going to rest until I understand what you've done."

He wasn't planning to let Marsh rest either. He watched, hoping this was enough to rattle the fake medium without revealing his own position.

The other man only gazed back, slightly surprised, perhaps, but no longer trembling or pale. God, Court had dealt fairly with plenty of men with no conscience. He'd always followed the rules, but something had turned that day Lily died. Still, he knew he couldn't, wouldn't cross certain lines. Whatever happened, he would bring this man to justice. Anger made the pulse in his forehead throb.

"Let me tell you something, Marsh. I was out to discredit you, but now I want to do more. I want to bring you all the way down."

Marsh's brows knit. He looked truly confused. "You were sent by whom?"

"It's my job." He pulled out the badge.

Marsh made a soft gulping sound, as if he was about to be sick. "You're a copper?"

Court tucked it away without answering. He didn't think the man would gibber and confess, but a little fear of God in the watchful form of Her Majesty's authorities might make him careless.

Marsh threw back his head and began to laugh. "Peeler. God almighty. You named yourself after Robert Peel, didn't you? No wonder I couldn't find a thing about you. Your first name's Robert."

Court scowled. This was not the reaction he'd expected. The other man's stiff wariness had vanished at his revelation. He'd intended to bring Marsh to a panic or at least a rage.

Marsh still grinned. "You're a copper. I should have guessed it, hey? You have the stiff-arsed bearing of one. Thank God for that."

Now Court was the one thrown into confusion. The man was far too cool. He should be more nervous, not relieved. He grabbed Marsh by the lapels of his checked coat and hauled him forward. The smile vanished, replaced by something else. Not fear. Those parted lips spoke of anticipation. Hell, no, he'd ignore that.

"I don't know what is so amusing, Marsh. But I'll find out. I'm going to discover every secret you ever held."

One of Marsh's eyebrows quirked. "Perhaps we share some of those secrets?"

Court understood at once. Marsh was suggesting they shared the predilection for men. He immediately let go of his jacket, heart pounding as if he'd run after Marsh.

The carriage drew to a stop. "This is your lodging?"

Marsh gave him a cool look as he smoothed down his lapels. "You know that, don't you, inspector."

Of course he knew, but that last comment Marsh had made, the one about shared secrets, had thrown Court into a state of alarm. He should have been amused that the man he'd set out to intimidate and trap had tossed him into a strange maelstrom of confusion. He might have been amused except—

Lily.

Court had no interest in allowing a criminal, a possible murderer, to gain the upper hand. Base attraction must be overcome.

He forced himself to look Marsh up and down and sneer slightly, as if what he saw was not worthy of remark. The memory of Marsh leaning on him, that scent of him, none of that sort of nonsense would be allowed to intrude. And his own secrets would not enter into the matter. "Yes. I do know this is where you live."

Marsh opened the door and climbed out. He began to shut it behind him. Court grabbed it and pushed it open so hard that the carriage swayed and the horse shuffled back a few steps. Court leaped down onto the pavement and faced the psychic.

"You are going to invite me in for a cup of tea, Marsh. We're not finished with our conversation yet."

Marsh stared at him, those strangely luminous eyes practically glowing in the light of the streetlamp. No wonder his dupes believed he possessed otherworldly gifts. Something about his gaze made a person feel he could see right into the hidden recesses of a soul.

He dipped his head. "Very well, Mr. Peeler. Perhaps I can lay your fears about me to rest." He held out a hand, gesturing to the faded front door of the shabby, terraced house. "Welcome to my humble lodgings."

He was in for it now. A policeman coming in for tea—what an excellent ending to a horrible evening.

Well, at least Lady Markham had paid his sitting fee. There was that. And Robert Whatever-his-name-was couldn't prove Oliver was a fake, since he'd done nothing legally wrong. But the inspector was an angry man, convinced Oliver knew something about a murder case and determined to prove it. That part was very, very bad. An angry cop could arrest a man on trumped-up charges or make him have to flee town fast, destroying the trust of the clientele he'd so carefully worked to build.

Also, Peeler had dismissed the cab, so he evidently intended to stay awhile. Not what Oliver wanted when his head still ached and his mind was in an uproar about the bizarre shift in reality he'd experienced.

As Oliver put the key in the lock, then led the way upstairs, he was acutely aware of Robert Peeler's presence behind him, the heavy tread of his footsteps on the creaking stairs, the heat of his body. Hell, if it was a different night with a different sort of man, he might be anticipating a good rogering before the night was through. But given the circumstances and the grim, angry man following him up the stairs, fun times were not on the schedule tonight.

Entering the room, Oliver turned up the gaslight and glanced around, looking for anything incriminating he might've left lying about. The sitting area with its worn carpet and shabby horsehair sofa and chair held nothing of interest—except the notebook in which he jotted notations about his marks, their backgrounds, family connections, deaths of family members or friends, and of course, whatever he could learn about their finances. One sitting like tonight's could lead to others, and he needed to know who was a good financial prospect to ingratiate himself with. Oliver felt like he'd swallowed a boulder, but he didn't allow his gaze to linger on the black book. He turned to his uninvited guest. "May I take your coat?"

Peeler surrendered his hat and coat grudgingly and Oliver hung them on the hooks near the door.

"Please take a seat, and I'll heat water for tea." As he moved toward the sofa, he inserted his body between Peeler and the notebook. The first opportunity he got, he'd grab it from the end table and shove it under the sofa before the cop noticed it.

"Don't bother about the tea. Sit down." The terse command should've angered or worried Oliver, and it did, but it also sent a quick fillip of arousal twisting in his groin. He couldn't resist the tone of a man in charge.

He obeyed, taking a seat on the sofa while Peeler stood before him like a headmaster questioning a wayward schoolboy. The man's clear gray eyes saw everything. There was no opportunity to hide the notebook.

"Please, take a seat yourself," Oliver offered again, gesturing to the chair across from him. But Peeler remained standing, towering over Oliver and intimidating with his height. It was a common trick but effective. Oliver felt intimidated.

"Where were you last Guy Fawkes Night?" the inspector asked bluntly.

"Last year? How can I be expected to remember what I did a year ago? Who is this Lily Bailey?"

"You know." Peeler suddenly bent over him, staring right into his eyes, jaw tensed so tightly the flesh drawn over it was white. "You have to know who she is, because you know what she said to me that night."

"Said to you?" Oliver repeated, and his fear that he could be dealing with a murderer reared its head again. Police inspectors could be killers as well as anybody.

"I was with her as she died. Head bashed in," he spat. "You repeated the last words she spoke to me. Only someone lingering nearby could have possibly done that."

"Lingering nearby?" Apparently he was incapable of doing more than repeating everything the man said. "Where? I have no idea what you're talking about, who this girl is, or where her death took place. I assure you I was nowhere nearby."

Peeler continued to glare into his face. Oliver experienced that insidious sense of guilt a person feels when fiercely accused of something even while knowing he didn't do it. For a moment, his brain froze. His natural ability to talk his way around any situation abandoned him. All he could see was Peeler's furious gray eyes, the harsh bones of his face straining against his taut skin, the grim line of his mouth that condemned him. He did not want to be on this man's bad side.

Then suddenly a switch flicked inside, and a thought occurred to him. "Last November fifth. Yes, I do know where I was, and I have proof that I was there." He jumped up from the hard sofa, nearly knocking Peeler backward.

Oliver headed for the small bookcase in the corner, surreptitiously seizing the notebook on the way past and shielding it with his body. The inspector might be interested in him for this murder, but he'd happily arrest him as a swindler if he had a shred of evidence.

After tucking the notebook between a pair of books, Oliver retrieved what he'd gone there for and returned to Peeler with it. "My scrapbook. I keep invitations, letters of thanks from clients, and recommendations. Showing these to new clients helps convince them of the validity of my abilities. I have here an invitation to Sir Abernathy's country estate." He flipped through the pages until he came to the embossed cards with the flowing script. He thrust the book at Peeler for his inspection.

"So you received an invitation. That doesn't mean you attended."

"You can contact Abernathy or any of the guests who were there that weekend. And his estate is miles from... Where did this murder take place?"

Peeler didn't answer. "I'll be certain to interview them if you give me a list of those who attended."

"Of course, but I have more proof right here. Read this." He turned the page to show the letter Abernathy had sent, thanking him for laying to rest his fears for his dead wife. Oliver had assured him she was content in the great beyond and that she forgave him his infidelities. Reassurance was a big part of his business. It was all most people really needed.

The letter was dated several days after the event and was a clear indication that Oliver had spent the entire weekend in the country. He watched Peeler's face, ready to gloat when that realization sank in. But those cool gray eyes remained distrustful as they swept back up to his face.

"Are you convinced, Mr. Peeler? By the by, what is your real name?" Was it Bailey, the name he'd used for that confounded Lily? But Peeler ignored his words and stared at him intently. At least the hostility and rage no longer glowed in those eyes.

"How did you know, then? You must tell me." He gave a mirthless laugh and in a less certain voice said, "And what did Lily mean by weak?"

Good. The man sounded as if he was on the edge of believing Oliver's power. Funny, because for the first time, Oliver was too.

"I..." Oliver was at a loss for how to play this. With most clients, he'd bluff his way through, tell them anything they needed to hear to make them believe him. But this was different. Tonight's experience had been real, and he finally understood that his grandmother and his great-uncle Paul he'd heard stories about might have been telling the truth when they got their flashes. "I don't know what to tell you, Mr. Peeler. What happened tonight was different from anything that's happened to me before."

Sometimes the truth was best. Let the inspector make of it what he would.

"You're saying you had a genuine psychic experience tonight? That you heard a voice from beyond telling you what to say?"

"Yes. Something like that." Oliver paused and recalled the experience. "Although it's not really an audible voice. I'm in that moment." Which had actually been fairly unpleasant, like having uninvited bats flitting around in one's belfry. Not to mention the terror that filled him. God. He reached for the drink.

"You say nothing like this has ever happened to you before," Peeler continued. "That statement means you admit you've been lying to your clients prior to tonight."

"Does it?" Oliver kept his pounding pulse under control and his tone as bland as rice pudding. "That wasn't what I meant."

"But it's what you said. I could arrest you on fraud charges right now."

Oliver suspected those were empty threats, but the big man might easily make his life a misery if he didn't take a stand. "I could deny what you think you heard me say. I have plenty of clients who would support my claims of communing with the dead. They've witnessed it."

"Most wouldn't wish to be revealed as true believers in a public forum, and a trial would ruin your 'business'."

Stalemate. Oliver paused for a moment, studying Robert Peeler's big, square hands holding the scrapbook. "What exactly is it you want from me, Mr. Peeler? I've told you the truth about what I know of Lily, which isn't much. What do you expect me to do now?"

Peeler looked up at him and slowly closed the book. "Tell me more."

## Chapter Three

Court watched Oliver Marsh, reading every emotion that flitted across those expressive eyes. The man might know how to lie and act sufficiently to fool his so-called clients, but he couldn't hide himself from an investigator. Court saw worry and uneasiness in his suspect but not the kind of panic that a man guilty of a violent crime might exhibit. Marsh's transparency, coupled with proof of his whereabouts the night of the murder, were enough to convince Court this man wasn't Lily's killer. But that didn't mean he had no prior knowledge of the murder and Court's connection to it.

Yet somehow Marsh had quoted Lily's exact words, which no one but Court knew. He hadn't written them down or repeated the exact phrasing to Childs, just said she'd murmured something about meeting Phillip.

He probably should have put every word she'd said in the official record, though neither Superintendent Hardy nor Childs had pushed for those details. But the precise words and their tone had been etched into his mind, never to be forgotten. Those details Marsh had captured were almost enough to convince him Marsh really was a conduit to something. Spirits? Visions? Court had trouble articulating the thought in his own mind—and didn't truly want to.

If he allowed himself to believe, the next logical step was to assume the other piece of information from Lily was true and might be a clue to her murderer's identity. This route of logic required a vast suspension of disbelief, but if he followed it to its conclusion, his next step must be to question Marsh again in his capacity as a medium. There might be more information that Lily would share.

"My God, I'm losing my mind," Court muttered, rubbing a hand over his brow. In the blink of an eye, he'd gone from being an avowed skeptic to a man actually considering requesting an audience with a dead woman. If a practical man such as himself could be swayed, no wonder sheep like Lady Markham and her set were so easily hoodwinked.

"You don't look well, Mr. Peeler. May I get you a drink? Something a little stronger than tea, perhaps?" Marsh reached into a cupboard beneath the bookcase and took out a bottle and two glasses.

Court's instinct was to decline the offer, but when the other man handed him the glass with a couple of fingers of brandy, he tossed it down. Marsh did the same. Court had the odd feeling that they were sealing some sort of unspoken deal. *A devil's bargain,* his mind whispered.

"Will you sit down? We can discuss this," Marsh said.

Court moved to the chair and sat at last, heavily. He was exhausted and wanted this evening to end. He didn't want to dredge up memories of Lily and the investigation he'd been forced to abandon, but here was someone who might hold a key at last, and he couldn't let the opportunity slip through his fingers.

Marsh refilled Court's glass and his own before sitting on the sofa facing him. "Please tell me more about Lily and what happened to her." His voice was low and inviting. Compassionate. No wonder he was such a good confidence artist.

"No. I think not," Court replied. "The more fact you know,

the more of the story you can invent. If your 'gift' is real, I'd like you to go into a trance right now and put me in contact with Lily."

Marsh frowned. "It's not that easy. It takes a group of strong-minded believers to, uh, set the right atmosphere. Besides, my energies have already been diminished tonight. I would need to rest and—"

"You can't do it," Court interrupted. "You *are* a fake."

"Simply because I can't perform on command doesn't make me a fake." Marsh's tone was sharp. For the first time, his irritation showed. "I would be happy to help you with your investigation to the best of my abilities, but not tonight. I need to rest now."

"And leave town while my back is turned. No. I think I'll stick close by you, Mr. Marsh, until I get what I need from you." The moment the words were spoken, Court heard a double meaning he'd never intended in them. He had no motive other than uncovering information for spending any time with Oliver Marsh. So why had other, earthier reasons leaped to his guilty mind?

Luckily, it appeared Marsh had divined no prurient suggestion. "I suppose I could try to enter a trance right now, but I wouldn't hold out much hope. One can't force the spirit world to cooperate with an earthly timeline."

"How convenient." Sipping his second glass of brandy, Court realized the alcohol was going to his head. A pleasant fog dulled his senses and took the edge off his tension.

"Sarcasm isn't helpful, sir." The medium rested his glass on one knee and tapped a finger against it. "Anxiety is hardly conducive to entering a meditative state."

"You're anxious, Mr. Marsh?"

"Why shouldn't I be? You've accused me of both murder

and deceit tonight. Yes, I'm a bit shaken."

"And from your strange experience." Court leaned forward, studying the other man's pale face. "Tell me exactly how it happened, what you felt, what prompted those words."

"I explained already. It's as if a presence was sharing my body and her words were pushed through my mouth." He licked his lips, then swallowed. There was fear in his eyes, but Court would wager it had nothing to do with his own presence. Marsh stared at nothing Court could see, and it terrified him. "I couldn't share her thoughts, only emotion and words. Some of the words she heard, perhaps? I don't know. They came out of my mouth like...like vomit."

Court narrowed his eyes and stared harder, searching for a sign of lying, some twitch that would show Marsh was prevaricating. But the man seemed utterly truthful—at least in his belief that he'd channeled a spirit. "Tell me the truth now. You've not experienced this before, have you? What happened tonight was a fluke."

The psychic hesitated, clearly not ready to tip his hand. "Nothing *quite* like this. It was very powerful and definitely beyond my control." He paused, then added, "I heard it like an echo. Though I think I also felt her...pain at being ripped from this world too early, and her astonishment that there were others. Other dead women, I mean. That's all."

Court exhaled a long breath in something like a sigh. The murderer was a man who'd killed more than once and who would hunt again? He prayed this was just Marsh's vivid imagination.

He was as exhausted as Marsh claimed to be and not in the mood to press for another séance. Perhaps he wasn't ready to hear what Lily might have to say—if her spirit existed at all and this wasn't some elaborate hoax. On the other hand, he didn't want to let this opportunity slip away."

He rose from the chair a bit unsteadily. "I'm going to leave now, Mr. Marsh, but I will return tomorrow to talk with you again. I trust I won't find you've left town in the night?"

Marsh rose and faced him. "No. I won't. I have appointments to keep, and my mother's expecting me for tea tomorrow. I will be busy most of the afternoon, but you might stop here at eight o'clock in the evening, and we'll pursue this."

He held out his hand to shake, and Court took it. The pressure of his clasp was warm and firm and lasted perhaps a few moments too long before Marsh let go. Court's hand tingled slightly, and he found himself wishing they were still touching each other. The subtle messages of physical attraction were something that could not be explored, not with this man, who was quarry of another kind.

If the situation had been different, Court would've been pleased to engage in a fast, rough coupling with the handsome man. But Marsh was a fraud suspect and a possible link to solving Lily's murder. Sexual contact should be the furthest thing from Court's mind.

Unfortunately, it wasn't.

He cleared his throat and moved toward the door. Marsh handed him his hat and coat. "Tomorrow evening, then. I honestly hope I can help you."

His tone was sincere, and Court believed him. "I hope you can too."

# Chapter Four

The following morning, Oliver cancelled his afternoon appointment with Cubby Baker even though the man was one of his most faithful clients. Cubby would always seek him out for more reassurances from his dear departed mother that he was following the path she'd chosen for him and that he was still the light of her heart. Cubby was a perpetually devoted son with no marriage prospects in this or any other life.

After the upsetting evening and a restless night's sleep, Oliver couldn't have stood listening to Cubby's whining at any rate, but more importantly, he had to take a trip to the library to read back issues of the *Times*. He must find out everything he possibly could about the Lily Bailey murder before his meeting with Robert Peeler—or whoever he was—tonight. If he couldn't rouse Lily's spirit, he needed to have some patter to offer the detective.

*Playing with fire*, his inner voice warned him. *You should leave town before you get caught in a trap.* But where could he go that the determined Peeler wouldn't find him? Besides, he couldn't abandon his mother, who was dependent on him not only for the money he provided but for an occasional visit. No. Somehow he'd find a way out of this jam with his business intact.

*Maybe it's time to abandon the psychic game*, the helpful voice murmured. *He can't make a case against you if you stop now. Find a legitimate line of work.*

Unfortunately, nothing paid so well as Oliver's consultations and séances. He'd inherited no shop or business from his father, only debt. Every line of work he'd considered, he'd already understood would not suit him.

He couldn't imagine the mind-numbing boredom of sitting in an accountant's chair from dawn to dusk, but he suspected his trouble was more than simple boredom. He'd had a severe headache the three days he worked for a merchant and nearly passed out for the short time he was employed as a clerk in a bank. "You are too womanly," his mother's friend had said, scoffing. "No physical strength."

Oliver had considered dragging the old fool outside and showing him his strength. But the old humbug was company for his mother, who longed to return to the country, and Oliver had long ago learned to ignore the jibes. His grandmother had been the same, his mother told him, and a long-dead uncle couldn't even bear to live in the city.

The truth was Oliver was very good at what he did—listening to people and helping them find peace in their lives. The work paid well. As long as he stayed in rooms with fewer than twenty people, he seemed to be all right.

He dressed and locked up his rooms, then walked down the street to a nearby shop, where he had a cup of tea and a bun. He missed the wonderful café he used to frequent during his brief time in Paris. Those had been lovely, halcyon days with late-morning lovemaking followed by a stroll to the café where he and Maurice would while away the rest of the morning. Unfortunately, his short-lived love affair had been far more tempestuous than that romantic interlude in Paris.

When it was over, he'd returned to London, broke, unemployed and facing the imminent death of his ailing father and a mother counting on him to save her from the family's ravaged finances.

Almost like a psychic vision, the idea of doing readings was born one day as he glanced through the newspaper and saw an advertisement for a renowned mentalist performing on stage. *This is what you should do,* the inner voice that usually guided him to wise choices—if he'd listened to it, he wouldn't have skated off to France with Maurice—whispered to him. Oliver heeded the voice, read all he could about the Spiritualist movement and about how mediums operated. He went to a few séances as well as private readings, listened to the hucksters' patter, observed their tricks, shaking tables, flickering lights, sepulchral voices, and he knew he could do better.

People had always been drawn to him and easily confided in him. His mother used to say he could charm the feathers from a goose, then get the goose to stuff a mattress with those feathers. Oliver applied his investigative and skill at reading character and set himself up as a medium—complete with calling cards. Damned if he'd let Robert Peeler pull down all that he'd worked so hard to build. He would not give up his business.

Oliver had never used props such as strings to move objects, because such contrivances were easily discovered. He operated purely on the strength of his personality and on his clients' desire to believe in him and in the afterlife. Whether Oliver had any actual ability or not, Peeler couldn't prove fraud.

Oliver was sweating from his vigorous walk by the time he reached the London Library on St. James. This was hardly his first time checking back issues of the *Times* to learn details about potential clients. His subscription to the library was well worth the cost. The librarian who worked in the archives greeted him by name and went to fetch the newspapers for the requested dates. Oliver sat in the reading room and skimmed the issues, searching for murder cases featuring young women and for the name Lily.

When her name in black and white leaped out at him, his heart stuttered. Lily Bailey was a real person, a young woman slain by a killer. She had been "interfered with" as the journalist so delicately put it. Raped. Before the murder or after? Or maybe during? Oliver winced.

A nightmarish sense of unreality flooded him. He had felt Lily. There was no point in pretending the episode at Lady Markham's house was some passing flight of imagination. Something real had touched him. This wasn't exactly the first time he'd had a glimpse of the mystical. He'd had glimmers of knowledge or feelings before. But this was the first full-blown channeling he'd ever experienced. Too bad his grandmother wasn't still alive so he could talk to her about it. Or even crazy Great-uncle Paul. But both of them were deceased.

Oliver shook off his shock and concentrated on the article, searching for clues to Robert Peeler's identity. The vilely slaughtered victim had been discovered by a relative before she'd expired, one Mr. Robert Court. Could it be that easy? Court instead of Peeler?

He shivered when he read that the man in question, Mr. Court, was a detective summoned to the scene of a crime only to discover the victim was a beloved relation. She roused for several seconds, then fainted, never to regain consciousness.

Oliver finished scouring the article for possibly useful details about Lily; then he read through the succeeding days' papers, learning about the arrest of a suspect and his trial. It sounded as if the halfwit dustman named Peter Dolittle had been in the wrong place at the wrong time. He'd been near the scene. Police had questioned and apprehended him, and he'd been railroaded along to the gallows. Poor Mr. Dolittle.

*It wasn't him.* Oliver felt a sense of menace that didn't come from a skinny slack-jawed individual like Dolittle. The flickering sense of the man was of someone larger and less ragged. And the emotion? Thought? No, neither of those. Whatever was invading his mind didn't seem to come from the usual internal voice. In fact, Oliver wasn't certain this was his own thought at all. The sense of unreality returned to him, as if he were floating at a remove from his body, watching himself sit at the library table and stare at newsprint. While part of Oliver was in a trancelike state—calm, attentive, listening—a goodly portion of him was running to the door and pounding on it with both fists and crying, "Let me out!" He did not want to be trapped in his head with a dead girl. At least this time her words didn't come pouring from his mouth, so, even in this haze, he understood he was gaining some control.

The moment passed, and he could breathe again. He was alone at a table in the library, and his body trembled with the passing fear that wasn't his—or at least not entirely his. This incident was not as consuming nor as terrifying as the episode in Lady Markham's, but now he couldn't deny the fact that he had some sort of dreadful skill to see the violent past.

Now he must decide what he would do with this ability.

He didn't want to become further involved with Robert Peeler—or Court, the very man who was trying to defame him. But he knew intuitively that Lily Bailey was not going to stop invading his mind until he helped solve her murder.

Besides, if he was being honest, there was a part of him, mostly located between his legs, that *did* want to meet with Robert Court again. From the moment Oliver had woken from his swoon in the man's arms and looked up into those serious gray eyes, he'd been attracted. If circumstances had been different, the evening might have ended in a tryst. In fact, that was rather where Oliver had assumed things were going when the stranger had offered to make sure he arrived home safely.

But even after Court had revealed his vocation, flashing his badge and talking tough, Oliver had still been attracted. Maybe more so, since he loved a man in charge. That authoritative voice and brusque manner had aroused him greatly. So yes, he wouldn't completely mind seeing the detective again this evening.

Oliver glanced at his pocket watch and realized he'd lost most of the day to reading. No matter how he hurried, he'd be late to tea at his mother's house. Nevertheless, he put the papers in chronological order before returning them to the librarian. It was important to foster goodwill with a source he used on a regular basis.

Outside, the promising sunny morning had been replaced by a gloomy British afternoon. Clouds threatened, and the air was misty, although the slight drizzle hadn't forced people to put up their umbrellas quite yet. Oliver hailed a hansom and rode across town to his mother's home on Rose Street. The floral name didn't reflect the shabby dullness of the neighborhood. After having to sell their family home to pay the bills left by his father, Oliver had helped his mother find lodgings in a more affordable neighborhood.

If he was truly a good son, he would've lived with her there and taken proper care of her, but given the somewhat questionable nature of his livelihood and of course, his sexual predilection, he needed his privacy. For that matter, maybe Mother needed her privacy too. He was fairly certain her gentleman friend, Mr. Wiggins, was quite close to her and sometimes stayed until late at night. Good woman that she was, she would've felt the need to keep this indiscretion from her son, if he lived with her, and would've been hard-pressed to carry on an affair. Better for them both to have private lives.

Oliver knocked on the door, and the day maid, Alice, answered. She bobbed a curtsy and took his hat, coat and umbrella. "Good day, sir. Fair weather we're having."

He smiled at her sarcasm. He liked Alice. The woman's salt had been good for his mother's dull life. Meek as a dormouse for as far back as Oliver could remember, Mrs. Marsh was finally developing some opinions and thoughts that weren't a reflection of her late husband. The change was long overdue.

"Mrs. Marsh and Mr. Wiggins await you in the parlor," Alice said. "Along with Mr. Wiggins's niece."

Oliver's brows shot up. His mother hadn't suggested there'd be any guests at tea.

"A quite young, *unmarried* lady." Alice tipped her head and gave him a look.

"Thank you, Alice." Oliver smiled, liking the maid more than ever for warning him that he was walking into a setup. He drew a deep breath before entering the parlor, where he greeted his mother and her guests with a brilliant smile. "So sorry I'm late. I was detained. I hope I haven't kept you all waiting for your tea. Mother, you should have warned me there would be guests... Not that I should keep *you* waiting either."

He bent over the tiny woman in the large wing chair and pressed a kiss to her cool cheek. Her skin had always been cool no matter how hot the day might be or even if she sat beside the hearth. And she always smelled like lilacs. He felt a surge of affection for her familiar quirks.

"How are you?" he asked as he pulled away.

"Very well, son. I should like to introduce you to Mr. Wiggins's niece, Miss Carol Hathaway." She rose, and the squat gentleman and willowy young woman, sitting on the other chair and sofa, rose too.

Oliver shook hands with Wiggins, then bowed over the Hathaway girl's hand. "Pleased to meet you." He spoke politely, neutrally. There were times when his ability to charm was useful. This wasn't one of them. The slightest hint of interest and his mother and Wiggins would be pushing the girl at him relentlessly.

"Pleased to meet *you*, Mr. Marsh." The girl's bright eyes assessed him and clearly found him acceptable. Oliver was quite surprised her uncle would put him forth as a prospect, knowing the Marsh family's financial straits and how Oliver earned a living. Maybe the Hathaways' situation was even less desirable.

"I've just moved here from Leeds, so it is a pleasure to be introduced to someone. My mother and I have moved in with my uncle, and we don't often go out." Her accent was only slightly tinged by the north. She'd had an education, was a young lady, but not as coddled as other girls her age.

Something was bothering her. Oliver didn't know exactly how he understood this, but he'd had this sort of flash of understanding of another person's situation off and on most of his life. This was a useful ability—unlike the moments he'd been invaded by Lily's presence.

Oliver nodded. "It is hard to adjust to living in a new place." And now he was burning with curiosity about why Miss Hathaway had moved to London to live with her uncle. Had her family fallen on hard times? Or were they hoping for better marriage prospects by sending her to the city?

"Oliver knows about moving around. He spent some time on the continent," his mother said. "In France. Although how he managed to put up with their foreign ways, I don't know."

"It's only across the channel, Mother. Not like traveling to the wilds of Africa." But she was right, the rhythm of life in Paris had been very different from here. "Anyway, that was years ago. I'm certain you will find your new life in London enjoyable, Miss Hathaway."

"Particularly if I meet new friends such as you, Mr. Marsh."

He returned her bright smile with a paler version, determined not to encourage her interest.

Alice stuck her head in the doorway. "Shall I serve the tea now, ma'am?"

"Yes, please, Alice." His mother rose and ushered them all to the dining room, where Alice had laid out a lavish assortment of cakes and biscuits.

Oliver held Miss Hathaway's chair as she sat, and Mr. Wiggins performed the same service for Oliver's mother. Small talk and pleasantries occupied the next excruciating hour. Oliver was hard-pressed not to keep checking his watch. But at least the food was good. He tipped a wink at Alice when she returned with a fresh pot of tea.

"Delicious as always, Alice. Thank you." He offered his appreciation for more than the meals and housecleaning she provided. His mother would be lost without Alice. There'd been a period after Father's death when his mother would lie in bed around the clock. When Oliver had hired Alice, she'd brought his mother out of her lethargy and back to life. Shortly after that, Mrs. Marsh had met Mr. Wiggins at the home of a mutual acquaintance, and now she was a changed woman.

Oliver knew firsthand what grief could do to a person—even when they were grieving for someone who didn't deserve their devotion. That was why he knew exactly how to deal with his mourning clients.

"How is your…business?" Mr. Wiggins hesitated before the word, as if not certain whether Oliver's work qualified as real employment.

"Quite well." He kept his answer brief.

"Oliver is a medium," his mother explained to Miss Hathaway. "He has the ability to communicate with those who have passed on as my mother and aunt both had. Back in their day, such an ability was considered an embarrassing family secret. These days it is celebrated as a gift. Oliver has held séances in the homes of some very distinguished members of society."

"That is fascinating, Mr. Marsh. How do you do it?" Miss Hathaway leaned toward him with wide-eyed eagerness, acting as if her uncle hadn't already informed her of Oliver's profession, which was highly doubtful.

He wasn't at all in the mood to run through his usual spiel about the gauzy veil between worlds and the voices that spoke to him—especially now that he'd actually experienced it. The gauzy curtain was more like a nausea-producing sledgehammer—but all of them were looking at him expectantly. Oliver adopted his far-seeing look and unspooled a skein of philosophical rambling to keep them happy through the remainder of teatime. Afterward, his mother asked him to continue to visit with the guests in the parlor, but he made his excuses.

"I have an important appointment with a client who needs to communicate with his deceased cousin," he said truthfully. "I will see you next week, Mother. Perhaps I can take you on a stroll in the park, if the weather permits."

She lit up, and another rush of affection for her swept through him. "That would be delightful. If Mr. Wiggins and Miss Hathaway could join us, it would be quite an outing."

Oliver's smile froze. Despite his indication that he wanted to see only her, she seemed determined to push him together with this chit. "I'll send you a note." He bowed over the Hathaway girl's hand. "So good to meet you."

After a kiss on his mother's cheek and a handshake with Wiggins, he was free to leave at last. Alice waited at the door with his outerwear. "Have a lovely evening, Mr. Marsh. Keep yourself safe."

Oliver looked at her, a bit surprised by the warning tone of her words, particularly given that he wasn't feeling very safe going into this meeting with Peeler—or rather Court. "I will. And you look after my mother."

"I always do."

He hurried home as the shadows lengthened. With every footstep, his anxiety, which had simmered on a back burner all day, grew stronger. Robert Court would expect him to enter a trance on command and contact Lily again. Oliver was afraid he couldn't do it but was even more afraid he could. He didn't like the sensation of having his mind invaded. He didn't want to feel the dead girl's sorrow again.

Mingled with his fears was extreme excitement at the prospect of seeing Court again. What in the world did *that* mean? A stocky, muscular body, a rough-hewn face and pale gray eyes didn't add up to an exceedingly handsome man, and yet there was something about Court that woke Oliver up like a slap to the face. He wanted to hear that brusque voice again and look into those eyes, even though the man was his enemy out to destroy him. Innate attraction drew him to the tough detective, and Oliver's heart beat with anticipation as much as fear as he rushed toward his flat.

# Chapter Five

Court walked with his shoulders hunched, head bent low and hands jammed into his coat pockets as he strode toward Oliver Marsh's flat. The afternoon mist had turned to a steady drizzle, and he'd left his umbrella at home. He should've taken a cab, but he'd decided to walk, since he was already so close to Northhampton Square. Ironic that the scene of Lily's murder wasn't many streets away.

He'd visited the site today as he had so many times before, staring at the spot and examining every cobblestone, every brick in the surrounding buildings, every lamppost, doorway and window frame as if the location would give him the clue he needed to find her killer. But now, nearly a year later, the rusty stain that marked the pool of blood beneath her body had long ago washed away. There was no indication a murder had even taken place in that quiet back street.

Superintendent Hardy would've told him he was spinning his wheels in a quagmire of mud, searching for something that wasn't there. Inspector Childs would've reminded him the killer had been found, tried and hanged, and he should allow Lily to rest in peace. Recently Court had nearly begun to believe them. It had been some weeks since he'd even looked into his investigative file.

But Lily *wasn't* resting in peace, was she? If Marsh wasn't a scam artist, then Lily was rattling around inside the medium's head and trying to send Court a message.

Marsh. He took a moment to dwell on the man who'd turned his life upside down in more ways than one. In addition to reigniting Court's fire to find a killer, Marsh had ignited other things inside him—attraction, heady lust, the desire to touch...

Court prided himself on keeping his appetites firmly under control, satisfying them only very occasionally and with utmost discretion. He did not like the way Marsh sent longing racketing through him. The mere thought of Marsh's bowed upper lip, his soft brown waves of hair, the soothing tenor of his voice and those damned unearthly blue eyes was enough to make his cock rise.

Court willed it to calm. Damned if he'd let this young man have such control over him. He must be clearheaded tonight as he observed Marsh channel Lily—if Marsh even *could* channel Lily. He must be wary and clever, not ensnared in a web of lust.

Rain dripped off the brim of his bowler. A few drops landed on his nose, and he brushed them away as he entered the door of Marsh's building. His heart beat faster as he climbed the narrow staircase leading to the man's apartment. The air was dank and musty-smelling, and it was nearly as cold and damp inside as out.

Court knocked on the door and listened to the thud of footsteps crossing the floor. He caught his breath just before the door opened. Marsh's fine-featured face was as he remembered it—pretty. If he was a girl, Court would've described him as winsome, for there was something inherently charming in Marsh's manner. His eyes and smile drew one to him.

Marsh dipped his head. "Mr. Peeler." He held out his hands to take Court's dripping hat and coat.

Court glanced around the room, comparing it to the previous evening, wanting to see if Marsh had removed anything he thought might be incriminating. It looked the same, though perhaps slightly neater. His gaze swept over Marsh, taking in the sharp cut of his gray coat, the muted colors of his paisley waistcoat. He still dressed the dandy but more subdued than in yesterday's eye-burning checked coat.

Marsh hung his coat, then handed him a bit of toweling to dry off with. "The afternoon is damp," he remarked.

"The rain's diminishing." Court moved past him to the chair his host indicated, the same he'd occupied last night. A small table with a lit candle on it sat between the chair and the sofa.

"I'll pour you a cup of tea to warm you up." Marsh removed his jacket before going into the small kitchen. When he returned a few moments later with the tea tray, his shirtsleeves were rolled up to the elbow. The muscles in his forearms flexed slightly as he set the tray down, and Court couldn't stop watching his deft hands as he poured them each a cup and presented one to Court.

Fragrant steam rose from the cup, bathing his icy face. He sipped the scalding brew, then placed the cup on the edge of the table. "How do we begin? No tricks of the trade or setting an atmosphere. If you can really commune with the dead, show me."

Marsh nodded and put his own cup aside. "First we must be honest with each other. If you wish to hear from your dead relative, you must at least give me your true name."

"Why is that necessary? I told you, the more facts I feed you about either myself or Lily, the more likely you'll invent some fiction to appease me."

If Marsh was irritated, he didn't betray it by more than a slight tightening of his lips. "Shall I continue to call you Robert Peeler, then?"

Court hesitated. There was still the fraud investigation to

consider, but his undercover persona was already destroyed with Marsh. He should stick with the pseudonym, yet he suddenly found himself blurting, "Court. You may call me Court."

"Mr. Court." Marsh looked at him with a small, grave smile. He inclined his head as if accepting the name. "And I'm still Oliver Marsh. I don't have a hidden identity or a hidden agenda. The service I provide to my clients is real—I comfort them about the afterlife. I reassure them. There is no harm in what I do."

Court bit his tongue. There was plenty he could say about taking money from grieving people for pretending to pass on messages from their departed loved ones, but tonight he was here as a believer himself. Or mostly a believer. It seemed apparent *something* otherworldly had happened at that séance. "I'm ready to see if you are the genuine article. We should find out if you can make it happen again."

"I'm not sure." Marsh blushed.

"Go on," Court said. "You don't know how to establish a true connection to the dead, do you?"

Marsh ignored him. "It would be good if you had some personal possession of the girl's I could hold. I should've asked you to bring something."

"I brought a photograph." Court went to where his greatcoat was hung and took the tintype from the pocket. He returned to his seat and handed it to the medium. "My cousins, Lily and her older sister, Rose. She's the one on the left."

Marsh studied the photo. "Lovely girls." He glanced up at Court. "If I forgot to say it last night, I'm dreadfully sorry for your loss. A death in the family is hard enough, but murder..."

"Yes. Thank you." Court cut him short. "So, will that help? Can you begin now?"

Marsh set the photo on the table beside the candle. He

nodded at Court's teacup. "Could you set that on the side table, please, and then take my hands."

Court obeyed, removing the cup and hesitating only a moment before grasping the other man's hands. They were warm and dry and slender in his grip. Long fingers wrapped around the backs of his hands, palm slid over palm, and Court fought back the tingle of excited anticipation that shot through him. His body reacted beyond his control, imagining he was there for some other purpose. He steadied his breathing and concentrated. "Now what?"

Marsh's lashes shielded his eyes. "We wait," he murmured.

Court closed his eyes too. The room around them was so quiet he could hear every creak and groan of the wooden structure and the scratch of rodent feet in the space above the ceiling. The sofa was a little too far from the table on which their joined hands lay, forcing him to stretch to maintain his grip on the medium's hands. He shifted to ease the growing strain on his back. Was this Marsh's plan? Make Court so uncomfortable that he broke the connection before Marsh could enter a trance? Use the interruption as an excuse for not being able to perform?

Court exhaled slowly. His breath sounded loud in the silent room. He eased his grip on Marsh's hands and listened to the soft click of the other man's throat as he swallowed. How long was this supposed to take? At all of the séances he'd attended, the mediums generally got to it in a reasonable length of time so they wouldn't lose their audience's interest.

"I'm..." Marsh's voice made Court start. "I can't... I don't feel her. I'm sorry." He pulled his hands away from Court's.

Court opened his eyes. Marsh's face looked pale and strained, his brow furrowed and his eyes dark. "I did feel something before. Last night and then again today when I was—

"

"When you were what?" Court prompted.

The medium hesitated before speaking. "At the library. I was reading about the case in old newspapers, trying to find out what I could about Lily...and about you. She was there. Not in the library, in my head."

"So where is she now? If you're trying to convince me you're not a fraud, you aren't doing a very good job. I would've expected a better show than this." Court couldn't disguise the sarcasm in his tone.

Marsh cocked his head. "Is that what you wanted, a show? I thought you'd come for some real answers."

He drew a breath. It was easy to unleash his mistrust in Marsh's claims, but the man was right; he'd believed enough to come here for this reading. For now, he must put any doubts on hold and pursue this thing as if he was a true believer.

"All right. How can we put you in the proper frame of mind or compel her to come?"

"There's no compelling about it. It happens or it doesn't." Marsh picked up the tintype and studied Lily's image again.

Court looked, upside down, at Lily's curly hair and sweet smile. The photo had been taken several years ago. She was older now—*had been* older when she'd died, but still bright and innocent and too trusting.

A thought occurred to him. "You said touching one of her possessions might help you to connect with her."

Marsh shrugged. "I was guessing," he said softly. Oddly that hesitant admission did more to convince Court that, for once, he wasn't dealing with a confidence artist. He leaned forward in his chair and allowed himself to brush his finger over the photo and the fingers that still held it. "What if we returned to the site of her murder? If she were to haunt any spot, I'd think it would be that one."

Marsh put the picture down. "I suppose so. It's worth a try." As he rose, he added, "I do mean to help you if I can, Mr. Court. And I shan't charge a fee."

Court studied his earnest face and wondered how much of Marsh's desire to "help" was in hope that Court would then leave him and his shady soothsaying business alone. But he nodded curtly. "I believe you."

The two men put on coats, gloves and hats, Court's still dripping water, and headed down the stairs to the street.

The air was cold and clammy, although it was no longer raining. Court walked quickly, determined to get this over with as soon as possible. He could hear Marsh's fast breath behind, but neither spoke until they reached the spot.

The day was drawing in, and few people came near this quiet backstreet. No wonder the killer got away without any witnesses seeing. The closest neighbor was a small church and its moss-covered gathering of gravestones that huddled near the building.

He imagined the killer had fled after the deed but not far. Perhaps he'd waited, hunched behind that church's wrought-iron fence, and he'd watched until the police gathered at the scene. No doubt he'd hoped they'd count her death as an accident. He'd wondered if the murderer had been spooked by someone or something, because he'd left before making sure she was truly dead.

"Here?" Marsh's voice brought him back.

Court pointed at the cobblestones of the street next to the black lamppost. The mist rising from the stones might have been the wisp of Lily's ghost.

"She lay half in the street. Her head was... The back of her head was a mess." He stopped himself.

Marsh watched him, wearing that appealing air. *"You can trust me,"* those big eyes said. *"Speak and allow the pain to escape you. I will share your burden."* No wonder he was a successful confidence trickster. People were soothed by that look of intelligent interest, and they'd spill the secrets he'd use for his work. Communing with spirits.

Court rubbed the back of his neck and wished he was enough of a skeptic to just walk away from Marsh and his blue eyes.

Marsh dropped to a squat. He pulled off his dark glove and laid his hand directly on the damp stones. He closed his eyes and drew in a long breath, as if the scent of coal fire and old wet leaves and the graveyard could help pull out...whatever had caused those words that spilled from his lips.

He rose to his feet, shaking his head. "Nothing," he said and stepped back. "Shall we go?"

Before Court could answer, Marsh's eyes closed again. He moaned, the harsh noise loud in the quiet street. Something fluttered in the bush next to the church. He opened his eyes, but they were unfocused. He stared at nothing in front of them.

"There." He pointed at the graveyard. "There. Oh, God. I don't have the words for her, but I saw this time. I saw. She's wearing green." He still shook his head but quickly now, as if in denial.

Court remembered the exact shade—she'd been in a malachite green gown that day. Green, soaked in bright and dark red.

Marsh blinked. He stumbled forward and grabbed Court's arm, gripped it tight with his cold-reddened fingers. "Robert. Robert. There are others. He said so."

"Who is he?"

"I can't see. Did she know? I can't see it. She must not see it—him. Dizzy. Ugh."

Court covered the hand gripping him. "She's dizzy? Was it the blow?"

Under his fingers, Marsh's were cold and damp from the cobblestones—they trembled. Marsh breathed hard as if he'd been running. "Sleepy and sick."

Court was torn between the desire to haul the man into his arms to reassure him and to cuff him on the side of the head, demanding he—or Lily—give plain answers. He simply stood as still as possible, his hand on Marsh's. They must look an odd pair, Marsh gasping as if he was about to be sick, Court a wax figure neither going to his aid nor moving away.

"It's between seeing and feeling. No..." Marsh exhaled a long breath and hunched slightly as if he was collapsing in that breath, coming back to himself. His gaze was fixed on the ground at the exact spot where she'd lain. "There isn't logical, linear thought, so I can't ask questions. Jesus, how I wish I could."

Court recalled the séance. There were those blithe questions and replies Marsh had posed as he'd "communed with the spirits". This was entirely different.

"All right." Court squeezed the hand holding his arm in that firm grip. "Tell me exactly what you saw or felt."

Marsh raised his head. His eyes were filled with tears, but they didn't fall. He rubbed his coat sleeve over his face. When he straightened, he stumbled.

Without thinking, Court slid an arm around his shoulders to steady him. Marsh gasped, then gave a weak laugh. "Thank you."

"You're pale. We'll return to your lodging, shall we?" Court said soothingly. He hauled the other man against his side, trying not to enjoy the warmth and muscle under his arm. They began to walk, and after a few yards, the body against his stopped shivering.

Court could almost feel the strength returning to Marsh. He asked, "Why was she dizzy?"

Marsh gave a shuddering sigh. "I can't tell the why. I only feel her." He put his arm around Court's waist. Did the man notice how Court's step faltered at his touch? No, apparently he was too wrapped in his own thoughts. "It is like the wind. One can feel a breeze yet have no idea of its origin. Does the wind come from the angry trees? From the gods? The tides?"

"The earth's rotation," Court said without thinking.

Marsh twisted to look at him. "Truly?"

Court nodded and continued walking, feeling the gaze of the man but not returning it. He pressed his hand against Marsh's back to speed him up. Court wanted to get off the street.

"And that's the sort of thing they teach coppers, is it?" Marsh's voice was teasing now.

Court didn't answer. Truth was, he liked facts, especially when they fit together to add up to understanding something new—the puzzle part of his work.

Something warm landed on his wrist. He stopped and looked Marsh in the face at last. The other man's head was still turned toward him, inches from his. Too close. But the strange tension between them wasn't the only problem.

"Hell." Court came to an abrupt halt, staring at the trickle of blood that came from the corner of Marsh's mouth. A little came from his nose too.

Lily, he thought. She'd had blood too, much more of it. It had come from her nose, mouth and—he leaned back to look.

No, nothing trickled from Marsh's ear. That was a small blessing.

He pulled out a handkerchief from his pocket with his free hand and thrust it at Marsh.

"Blood," he said.

"Ugh." Marsh grabbed the cloth and covered his nose. "I apologize. I didn't know."

"There's no need." Court let go of him but stayed close. The pale young man might collapse to the pavement. "I think perhaps I should take you to a doctor. There's blood from your mouth too."

Marsh's forehead wrinkled. "I don't feel any pain. Very strange."

"Yes, well," Court began. He stopped. It was absurd to tell Marsh how for a second he looked too much like Lily. Even without the blood, Marsh slightly resembled the dead girl, though her eyes were never so beautiful and certainly her appearance never awoke the peculiar hunger deep in Court's belly. But that vulnerable haunted face... Court wanted to indulge the absurd need to grab Marsh now and protect him. He said, "Are you sure you don't need to visit a doctor?"

"I feel much better, actually. The dizziness was never truly mine."

"I shall accompany you back to your rooms," Court said.

Marsh finished wiping the blood from his face. He seemed about to hand the handkerchief back to Court but folded it and put it in his own pocket instead. "That's not necessary. I can return home without help."

"I think it is." Court wet his lips, trying to calm himself. "It would be my pleasure."

"Would it?" Marsh's brows rose.

Damn. His mouth went dry again. The signals were all there, coming strong from Marsh, the way he cocked his head, the way he allowed his gaze to linger on Court's mouth.

The strange episode, the blood that eerily mimicked hers—hell, simply recalling Lily's death—should have made Court think about anything but sexual frustration. Perhaps it was natural to wish to seize another person and celebrate the life force flowing through them.

This man who'd been shaking and pale had recovered so entirely, the rogue could even make vague propositions. They were quite the pair.

Court wondered if Marsh had any idea how much he, Robert Court, wanted to kiss him until they both moaned with unfulfilled pleasure. The slender white body stretched out under Court while he licked every inch of skin, working his way to the prize of the man's cock. The extravagant, filthy thoughts made him blush—and go hard.

Perhaps Marsh could do more than sense the horror of Lily's demise. He might be capable of putting such decadent images in Court's mind.

Court smiled at his desire—and his wish to blame that awakening desire on another man. No, the need to touch and taste Marsh belonged entirely to him. Every year or so, the hunger would rise up in him, take over his thoughts and sometimes even his actions, and he'd blindly seek out satisfaction.

He was used to it and usually allowed himself the sin of self-fulfillment, without regrets. Very rarely, he even touched another man and then, once satisfied, put the incident out of his mind. Guilt and shame were of no use to Court.

"What you cannot change, you must accept," his father used to say. Court suspected the old man knew of Robert's predilection and was grimly accepting. They loved one another in his family, though it would be absurd to speak of such matters. Almost as absurd as publicly stating he preferred men.

Marsh had been dragging, but now his steps sped up. He seemed preoccupied—hardly surprising. Court ventured, "You are rushing now. What are you thinking about?"

"Lily. That moment when it was too real. You."

Court waited, then prompted, "Me?"

"I was aware of you next to me and over me. All occurring at the same moment. I do not like it," Marsh added. "I hate it."

Court wondered if that meant he was discreetly telling him to back away from him. Leave him alone.

They approached the house. Marsh stopped and spoke softly. "The only time it is bearable is when you held on to me."

Court's step faltered. He caught up with Marsh, who was still speaking. "I was anchored then. The moment of horror is long over, I know, but it continues to echo through me and I wish... I want..." He let the words trail off. Marsh pulled out his key, unlatched the door. Court followed him up the stairs, their booted feet making a clatter on the wooden steps.

As soon as they entered the apartment, Marsh seemed to revive. He worked off his single glove. He undid the buttons of his coat.

Court stood in the middle of the floor, hands tucked into his coat pockets, waiting as he had just at the scene of Lily's murder. He would take his lead from Marsh.

"I am at your disposal," he said. Maybe Marsh would ask him to hold him again. It would be in the line of duty, so of course he'd accept. Court stifled a smile at himself.

"Give me five minutes," Marsh said and left him alone. Pulling his notebook from his jacket, Court walked over to a table and looked through the post piled there. There was nothing interesting, although Court scribbled down the direction and date of the engraved invitation. Marsh was to attend a country party in his capacity as professional medium.

When Marsh reappeared, his hair and face were damp, and all traces of blood were gone.

He reached into the cupboard beneath the bookcase and took out the brandy and the same two glasses he'd used the last time Court had visited. "I will talk as much as you want after I have a drink. Something stronger than tea this time. Would you like one?"

Court nodded. He pulled off his hat, coat and gloves and draped the coat over a chair. He was ready to listen. He might have harbored some doubts about Marsh, but he believed the man's connection to Lily, or at least her murder, was real. Shoving his gloves into his pocket impatiently, he wondered if this new acceptance of Marsh as authentic medium was his own body talking to him. He turned and examined Marsh. The more time he spent in the man's company, the more he craved him.

He knew too well a man might desire or even fuck a person he did not like, but Court always seemed to gravitate toward men he admired in other ways. Was he actually romantic enough to rewrite the truth in his head to match his lust?

"You are watching me with that look of condemnation in your eyes, Mr. Court. Don't you believe me?"

Court tried to relax the lines of his face and even attempted a smile. "I do believe you. I'm merely upset by the memories." It wasn't entirely a lie.

Marsh winced. "I beg your pardon. Of course what happened this evening was bound to bring back horrible memories of Lily's death. I am sorry."

His eyes grew bright, and Court already recognized that look he wore before saying something slightly outrageous. "I should be grateful that, for once, your grim look was not directed at me and my work."

He handed a glass of whiskey to Court.

"Cheers," Marsh said and downed several fingers at once. "You're welcome to ask more questions of me, but likely I know as much as you do. Perhaps even less. I was close to unconsciousness, or so it seemed to me. I don't know how much of what I felt was my own...and what was something else."

He reached for the bottle again. "It's the most damnable feeling, and I do not enjoy it, Mr. Court."

Marsh swallowed another glass down and then sat on the sofa. "Come sit with me," he ordered. "I think better when you're close. You're a solid sort of man, you know. Keep the nonsense at bay." He hiccupped gently.

Court walked over and sat at the far end of the sofa. "Perhaps you've had more than enough to drink."

"I'm not drunk," Marsh said and hiccupped again. "I'm not sure having you near is creating the, um. Desired effect. I am distracted, but now..." Without another word, he slid forward and slipped his arms around Court.

It was an unpolished move, rough and desperate. Nothing like the confident air of the medium.

"Hush, hush," Court said and patted his back as if he comforted a small child after a nightmare. "It's fine."

Marsh buried his face against Court's shoulder. His laughter was muffled and so were his words. "Oh, I didn't jump on you because of fear."

Court froze.

"I might be worse for drink after all. To do such a thing to a police officer. I risk prison, don't I?" Marsh's breath was moist against Court's neck and then his ear. His hand slid down Court's front. Court started as Marsh's hand brushed over his very stiff cock.

"But I won't go to prison after all, will I. I know the signs, Mr. Court. You want me." His chuckle brushed Court's cheek. "If I'm wrong, I beg of you, please don't beat me to a bloody pulp. If I'm right, oh, God bless. Yes." His mouth was on Court's, barely touching him with tentative, soft exploration.

Court raised his hands, placed them on Marsh's shoulders, bracketing his neck. He should pull the man off, away from him, but his fingers didn't obey. He stroked the side of Marsh's throat with his thumb. Then moved to his nape above the starched collar and threaded his fingers through his hair.

Marsh grunted—pleased triumph—and twisted to deepen their hesitant touch into a real kiss.

A shot of lust hit Court as if it had been a weight dropped from the sky to flatten him. He thought, *I do not have a prayer against such an enemy.*

Why enemy? He must think. If he gave in to this hunger, his power over Marsh as an officer of the law would be severely compromised.

He tried to recall Lily, to bring himself back to the reason he was in this room with Marsh. But instead of her broken body, he saw her alive, with an almost smug expression on her face. She smiled. *There's someone for everyone, even you with your tastes*, she'd once said. The only time anyone in his family had touched on the subject of his tastes.

Lily.

But, no. Jesus. She vanished from his thoughts as Marsh bit lightly on his lower lip, sucked it into his mouth, gently teased Court's tongue with his. The awkwardness was gone. The lithe young body under Court's hands moved closer. And then. God! Marsh was kneeling over him, his knees planted on the sofa on either side of Court's thighs. Marsh held his head and kissed and kissed him as he rubbed his torso on Court's rhythmically, and Court could feel the erection pressing against his stomach, just below his heart.

He swept his hands down Marsh's back and palmed his buttocks through tight trousers. He wanted to take control, to resurface to sanity, but the feel of the man's firm rear moving under his hands, the insanity of craving... Clear thinking was lost.

If he couldn't be in command of his thoughts, he'd take control of Marsh. He lifted Marsh easily, twisted and laid him on the sofa, lengthwise.

Marsh tried to scramble up, but Court was on him then, pinning him down with his body, kissing him on the mouth and cheeks, then back to his mouth. Marsh moaned into his mouth, and the sound, the friction created by their writhing, was almost enough to make him spend.

Not yet, no.

Court held Marsh by one shoulder and with the other hand unbuttoned his waistcoat, his shirt and the fly on his trousers. Enough access to the flesh he'd imagined. He imagined unwrapping Marsh more slowly as if he were a gift he gave himself, but now he was too impatient.

He let go of Marsh long enough to rear back and enjoy the sight of the man in disheveled clothing. He admired the stripe of pale skin against the flashy clothes, taking note of the hair on his belly and chest and the surprisingly large blunt head of his cock. Court had a good memory, and he was determined not to forget this moment. He'd treasure it during some long evenings alone.

Marsh began to sit up, and Court met him halfway, pressing him back down to the sofa.

"Unfair," Marsh said. "I would see you too."

"Soon," Court promised. Keeping one hand wrapped lightly around Marsh's throat to hold him in place, he kissed his neck, his collarbone.

Marsh exhaled a long groan as Court rooted through his clothes and discovered his nipple. Such a fine hard little bud. He sucked and enjoyed the flavor of sweat and sweet skin. He brushed his teeth over it and smiled as Marsh bucked up. A waft of his scent reached Court, making him even harder.

"Delicious," he said and continued to kiss his way down Marsh's flat belly. He stopped holding his neck, but Marsh remained obediently flat on his back.

"Good boy," he said.

"Huh." Marsh arched up again, fully uncovering his cock.

That was more than enough for Court. He took the heavy cock in his hand and tugged gently a couple of times. It was already damp with Marsh's eagerness but not quite wet enough to slide easily, so Court dipped his head and at last tasted what he'd hungered for for hours, perhaps since he'd first laid eyes on the man.

He closed his eyes and let himself enjoy the taste of Marsh on his tongue before plunging his mouth down over him. With one hand, he gripped the man's cock; the other went down his own trousers. He couldn't wait. He wouldn't.

"Do not deprive me," Marsh said. He pushed at Court's head, and Court looked up, licking his lips.

Marsh jutted his chin out, his gaze on Court's hand down his trousers. "Move closer. I want to touch you," Marsh said.

Court was going to point out he should ask nicely but decided he would save games for later. Now he slid off the sofa and knelt by Marsh, who reached over and deftly unbuttoned his trousers.

Very good. Marsh might touch him, and he could return the favor. He unbuttoned Marsh's trousers and with trembling fingers found his goal. He could easily pull Marsh into his mouth, lick and gulp at the treat of his cock. But it was large enough that Court had to keep a hand wrapped around the base to keep the eager Marsh from pushing too far. He'd done this with several other men and hadn't encountered such a beast as Marsh. The thought of such a cock inside him... But he didn't like that sort of activity.

He shuddered as Marsh stroked him—no one else had touched him for more than a year, and the exquisite feel of a warm hand on him, moving... *Harder*, he thought, and as if reading his mind, Marsh tightened his grasp. The hand moved faster, and for a moment, Court went still, concentrating on sensation.

Under his hands, Marsh bucked up, and Court returned to his delectable work. Too soon, he felt the familiar tightening, the tingle. He closed his eyes and tried to remember to move his hand, but his body was slave only to Marsh's touch. He groaned his warning just as the cock under his fingers grew impossibly hard and large. As the spendings touched his face and lips, his own orgasm struck. Each pulse brought him closer to losing his mind. He cried out, and the world grew faint.

God. After a few breaths, he rested his cheek on Marsh's sticky stomach. He could feel the fast beat of Marsh's heart through his belly and in the pulse of the shrinking organ that he still clutched.

Still on his knees at the side of the sofa, Court might be

worshipping the man he clutched and who'd brought him such shocking pleasure with just a few rubs of his hand.

Court tried to summon some disgust at the situation; he had abandoned that role he treasured. A sad failure of an investigator.

But instead of loathing, he felt a rare sense of peace. He could only look into the blue eyes that gazed back at him and smile.

# Chapter Six

*Beseeching eyes stared into his, begging him to help, but there was nothing he could do. His feet were cemented to the very cobblestones of the road, and he couldn't move, couldn't protect, couldn't save. He felt danger approaching like a terrible beast and strained to reach out to Lily...Marsh...Lily, to rescue her...him. Then abruptly the creature was there, tearing its victim apart, but Court couldn't see the beast, so he couldn't kill it.*

Court woke with a gasp, jerking upright and sucking in a deep lungful of air. The images of his nightmare were already dispelling like fog burned away by the sun, but the feeling of impending danger lingered. He swallowed. His throat was dry and his head throbbing from the aftereffects of too much brandy.

And he was not in his own bed.

Alarm of a different kind crashed through him as he registered a leg entwined with his and looked down at Oliver Marsh's brown hair, spilling over the pillowcase and tangled across his face. Court's momentary desire to brush back the other man's hair was immediately supplanted by dismay and the need to flee. He'd spent the night in Marsh's bed. He'd never meant for that to happen.

Marsh moaned softly and shifted, turning his head away and moving his arm so it cradled his head. Court took the opportunity to extricate his leg from underneath Marsh's and slip out of the bed. He stood for a moment, staring at the mussed bedclothes and the sleeping man; then he glanced down at his own half-clothed body. Buttons open, hooks and eyes unfastened, his semi-rigid cock lolling out of his trousers.

He trod lightly over the creaking floorboards and didn't put himself back together until he'd closed the bedroom door behind him. Then he hurried, tucking his cock into his drawers and buttoning the fly of his trousers, donning his shirt, waistcoat and jacket. His coat hung on the hook by the door. With a last glance around the room to make certain he hadn't forgotten anything, Court slid his arms into his coat, grabbed his hat and let himself out of Marsh's rooms. Only after he was halfway down the stairs did he remember he'd left the photograph of Lily and Rose behind, but that was all right. He could get it later.

The brandy had done this, he decided as he marched home with the speed of a foot soldier charging across a battlefield. He would own up to the sexual grappling he'd done with Marsh. No placing that at liquor's door. But spending the night curled around the other man for comfort? No. That was due to the soporific effects of too much brandy and getting chilled through on a damp, cold night.

After they'd finished satisfying each other, Court had intended to leave, but Marsh had poured him another glass to warm him on his way home. He'd drunk it in a few gulps, closed his eyes and let the alcohol heat him through.

Marsh had quietly asked him to lie with him for a short while. "I can't get Lily's memories out of my mind. Her terror haunts me."

Court could've pointed out that Marsh had appeared to banish those memories when they were busy pulling each other's cocks, but he'd simply nodded and followed the other man to his small bedchamber. Legs leaden and body weary, he'd been glad to lie down in the soft cocoon of Marsh's bed, wrapped in warm arms.

And that was the last thing he remembered until this morning.

Christ, poor Jock would be desperate for relief if he hadn't already piddled on the floor, and if the little terrier hadn't been able to hold it, he'd be shivering with shame and hiding in the broom closet or someplace.

Court spotted a cab idling by the edge of the road while the driver lounged on the box, drinking a hot beverage to drive back the morning chill. He hailed the driver and was soon rattling across town toward his house.

As he'd guessed, Jock was hiding rather than waiting with hindquarters wagging for his master to come home. Court whistled, and the small white dog slunk into the hall, head down and tail tucked.

"Poor little lad, it's all right. Not your fault I kept you waiting too long." He scratched the dog's chest until Jock perked up, clearly feeling forgiven, then clipped a lead to his collar and led him outside to do his business.

After that, there wasn't a moment to waste. No time for a cup of tea and definitely no time to mull over the events of the previous night. He was expected to check in at headquarters and give an update on his various cases. He'd be late for his meeting with Hardy as it was.

Court stripped off his sweat-reeking clothing and dressed in a fresh starched shirt, collar and trousers. His shoes could use a polish, but there wasn't time. He was buttoning his coat in the front hallway just as his housekeeper arrived. Mrs. Lally came over for only a few hours each day to give the place a general cleaning and make certain Court had at least one home-cooked meal a day.

"Sorry, Mrs. Lally. Jock had an accident someplace in the house. I haven't discovered where yet, and I've no time to look. If you don't mind..."

The sour-faced woman scowled but nodded. Court gave her a quick smile and slunk out of the house, feeling as shamed as Jock. Mrs. Lally had that effect on him.

A brisk walk got him to the station only ten minutes late for his appointment with his superior. But Hardy wasn't a man who tolerated tardiness and especially not from Court, whom he'd taken a dislike to.

The superintendent glanced up from the paperwork on his desk when Court entered his office. Hardy's drooping mustaches lent his face a disapproving air. His thick gray eyebrows furrowed into a frown when he saw Court. He held a pen in one beefy hand and pointed it at Court as if challenging him to a sword fight. "I've no time for you now, Mr. Court. My day is full. So rather than hear your reports verbally, I want a written update on your ongoing investigation on my desk by the end of the day. And I'll give you some advice. Finish pinning down this Oliver Marsh character so you can move on to another assignment. We've too many cases for you to take the amount of time you do on each one."

Hardy dropped his gaze back to his paperwork, summarily dismissing Court.

*Well, that was easy.* Court was actually pleased not to have to spend any more time than that with his supervisor, even if it meant having to write a few reports. He went to his desk, greeting a fellow inspector and two sergeants as he passed, and sat down heavily. He exhaled a long breath and wished he had a warm cup of tea at hand. His stomach was churning, and his nerves were frayed.

And he couldn't stop thinking about Oliver Marsh.

The man's intense eyes and caressing voice haunted him. Uncombed curls tumbling around that face—appearing so innocent in sleep—kept invading Court's inner vision. Snatches of memory popped up to torment him; panting breath, groans, naked flesh, flushed, rigid cock, hands touching him, stroking, moving him to ecstasy and—

"Court! Are you asleep?" Barry Baylor's booming voice broke his reverie. "I could use your help on the McCulligan case. I'm this close to pinning the bastard for all he's done, not just the whore-running but smuggling opium too, but I need help. Are you about finished playing parlor games with the ghost talkers? There are real criminals to be brought down."

"I can help you in my spare time. My current assignment doesn't take all my day. What do you need?"

"I don't know why he's wasting you on investigating those frauds at all." Baylor jerked his head to indicate the superintendent's office. "In my opinion, those Spiritualists get what they pay for, a fool's ride. If they're that naïve—"

Court might agree, but he wasn't about to point out he'd been unofficially demoted. "I'm well aware how you feel, but imagine if it were your mother throwing away her money and being duped into believing she could speak with her dead husband once more."

Baylor shrugged his big shoulders. "All I'm saying is it's not much of a crime. Not like the damnable opium that's pouring into this country. That's a real vice."

"Your point is taken." Court cut him off briskly. "But nevertheless I have to do what I've been assigned to do." *And was sleeping with the suspect part of the assignment?* He pushed that thought aside. "Now, what is it you'd like me to do?"

"Accompany me to the docks. There are a few men I need to

talk to, and I'd like backup." Baylor glanced across the room to where his sergeant, Fitzgerald, was laughing and joking with some of the other officers. "Not Fitzie. He doesn't have the, uh, appropriate investigative techniques. This is a delicate matter. The right questions have to be asked. If I wanted faces punched, I'd bring Fitzie."

"Right now?" Court regarded the files strewn across his desk and considered all the details he had to tend to today—in addition to writing reports for Hardy.

"Sooner would be better than later," Baylor said.

And so most of Court's morning was diverted to working on someone else's case, leaving him to scramble all afternoon to get his own work finished. He never had a chance to eat all day, and by five o'clock, his stomach was rumbling so loudly it made Peters, at the nearest desk, look up. The only good thing about being so busy was that it gave him no time to dwell on Lily's case. Or Marsh and all that had happened last night.

But as he walked back to his house at the end of the day, Court's mind turned like a compass needle back to Marsh and Lily. The two seemed inextricably linked now. He couldn't think of one without the other. Lily's death, Marsh's gift, and a possible solution to the mystery of who had really murdered his cousin—it was all mixed up together. *Along with flashing images of a sucking mouth, grasping hands, hungry eyes and oh, the sweet ache of his body pressed against Marsh's hard, agile form. How he'd like to push him flat to that mattress and pound into him, hard, harder, until the man cried out and begged for mercy. Ravage his mouth until Marsh was gasping for breath. Bodies trembling, aching, grunting, thrusting...*

Court blinked. He was standing before his front door and barely remembered the walk home. Inside the house, Jock was already welcoming him with sharp yips, and here he stood, as possessed by Marsh as Marsh was by Lily.

He should be concentrating only on the tiny scraps of information Marsh had revealed to him. It wasn't much. Only that Lily may have been drugged and that she believed her murderer had killed before and would again. It seemed almost as if she knew the man's identity and yet hadn't been able to reveal it. At least not through Marsh. Why did messages from the other side have to be so damned obscure?

All right, then. Let him retreat to a place of logic. If Lily *did* know her killer, how many men could possibly have been within the circumference of her life? She'd just moved to the city to be near her fiancé. She knew only the people her in-laws or Court himself had introduced her to. He should begin with finding out what introductions had been made and learning about each man. A year since the murder, the killer might be feeling secure. If Court was circumspect in his questioning, he might learn a great deal.

And as for Marsh...

Well, he'd have to see him again.

Even though Court had revealed his true identity, he could still keep tabs on what Marsh was up to, but beyond that, he would have no more dealings with the man. It seemed he'd learned all the medium was able to tell him about Lily, and as for the other... Best to stop that foolishness right away.


Oliver awoke with his head pounding and feeling as disoriented as a scarecrow after a gale. He dragged his heavy eyelids open and peered blearily around his room remembering two things—that something truly terrible and something profoundly wonderful had happened last night. But it took him a moment to remember what the two events were.

The terrible came first. Lily's impressions at the moment of her death crashed over him again, the dizziness and frustration at not being able to stop what was happening to her, the terror and the feeling of life slipping away. Loss, great aching, painful loss and longing for her family and fear as she faced whatever stood on the other side of the curtain. The one thing he hadn't received from her was an impression of peace and joy in the Great Beyond. Did that mean he'd been selling a load of hogwash to his customers all this time? A bright-colored fantasy to cheer their miserable lives?

He rubbed his forehead as if it would dispel the feelings or relieve his headache. And then the second part of the evening washed over him, infinitely more enjoyable if just as earth-shattering as his Lily vision.

Robert Court, that stocky bulldog of an investigator. A man he should fear, since he could bring his livelihood crashing down around him, and yet Oliver had clung to him like a life preserver in stormy seas. It was more than sexual attraction, although pure animal lust had definitely been a potent part of the mix. Oliver had enjoyed the frantic grasping moments as they brought each other to climax, but he'd loved wrapping himself around that solid body and sleeping together even more. Court had given him a feeling of security, an anchor to hold on to when his mind started to spin off into Lily's memories.

But now it was midmorning, and Robert Court had vanished without a word. Foolish of Oliver to feel a little hurt by that. He was certain the detective had never meant to stay as long as he did, but still it rankled that Court couldn't have poked him awake long enough to say he was leaving.

Now what would happen? If the man was embarrassed, ashamed or even angry at himself for indulging his desires, he might try to relieve those feelings by punishing Oliver. If Court had been determined to expose him before, their tryst might make the detective all the more rabid about ruining him. That kind of anger wasn't uncommon. Some men would fuck a man or boy on the street, then beat him senseless as if to exorcise their own perversion.

Oliver sat and winced as his head spun. Maybe he was being overly anxious. Perhaps Robert had merely left in a hurry to get to work. He'd be back sometime. They weren't finished solving Lily's murder, and right now Oliver was his only link to her, so he'd certainly want to talk to him again.

If only he could offer something concrete and usable. Perhaps Lily's message wasn't garbled, only his perception of it was. He was new to real psychic experiences, but his grandmother had supposedly lived with such flashes for years. He wished he'd asked her about it while she was still alive. Perhaps his mother might have some insight.

Oliver checked the time. It was still quite early in the day, hopefully too early for Wiggins to be there. He might actually get to speak to his mother alone if he went right now.

Groaning, Oliver climbed out of bed. He had no servant to do for him, so he pumped and heated his own water for washing up and brewing tea. As he washed his face, the flannel came away with a coppery stain, residue of last night's bloody nose. He'd felt no pain—other than the headache—before Court had offered him his handkerchief to mop up with. The bleeding was an odd phenomenon that he supposed had something to do with the spirit haunting him. He certainly hoped the experience hadn't caused some sort of internal hemorrhage.

Oliver fished the detective's crumpled kerchief from his coat pocket. There would be no bleaching those stains, and he imagined Court wouldn't want it back. He handled the square of linen and thought about its owner, a man by turns nurturing and forceful. He recalled how Court had slipped an arm around his back and supported him as they walked together, how he'd looked with concern at Oliver's bloody face and how he'd agreed without question when Oliver asked him to stay for a while since he was afraid to be alone. But the man was also tough, determined to see justice done not only in the matter of finding his cousin's killer but in ruining Oliver's business.

And that forcefulness transferred into a sort of roughness that Oliver quite enjoyed during their sexual dalliance. Oh, how he'd like more of that hard hand gripping his throat or pushing him down, and the strong pull on his cock, the almost painful sucking. He began to harden just thinking of it. Imagine having that big cock drilling into his backside. He winced and glanced down at his own cock, which was rapidly growing rigid.

Christ Almighty, one way or the other, friend or foe, he had to meet with Robert Court again. Had to see him and at least talk to him, but preferably more than that. He wanted him again with a fierce desperation that shocked him.

"Steady, boy," he warned himself; then he hurried to dress and trek the mile to his mother's house.

Alice answered the door and greeted him with her customary dryness. "Back so soon? I'm afraid the alluring Miss Hathaway isn't here today nor is her dear uncle." She all but rolled her eyes, and Oliver smiled at her cheekiness. Not everyone would appreciate such impertinence in a servant. He did.

"Good. It would be pleasant to have my mother to myself for once. Will you tell her I'm here?"

Moments later he was ushered into the sitting room, where his mother was crocheting one of her interminable doilies. "Son, what brings you here so early? If you wanted to join in the outing with dear Mr. Wiggins and Miss Hathaway, that was to be later this afternoon."

He leaned and pressed a kiss to her cheek. "No, Mother. I'm here to see you. I wanted to talk to you about Grandmother Silver."

"My mother?" Her eyebrows rose, and her hands stilled in her lap. "Whatever for?"

"Her gift and Uncle Paul's. I want to know more about it. Anything she may have told you about how it felt, what brought it on, and how she could control it."

"Mother never spoke to me about such matters. When she had a spell, we would tell the servants it was a migraine, but occasionally she would go into one of her trances in public and spout—oh, all sorts of things." She shook her head. "It was different in those days. Such bizarre behavior was considered a curse and certainly wasn't celebrated in the finest drawing rooms like yours is."

"Yes." He didn't know what to say. His poor naïve mother had believed in his abilities all along. How could he tell her that he had only now begun to experience real psychic flashes and didn't know how to control them?

"Would Grandmother have written any letters or perhaps kept a journal? There must have been someplace where she unburdened herself."

His mother's soft brown eyes glistened, and she swallowed. "It is difficult to speak of my mother. She and I were...so very different. We shared few confidences, particularly after I married your father, who was eager to distance himself from her 'mumbo jumbo', as he called it. But yes, I often saw her writing, and after she passed, I locked her diaries away along with some other mementos in a chest in the attic."

She paused and drew a shaky breath. "I never read them. It didn't seem right somehow, to pry into her private thoughts. But I feel now that maybe she was writing them for you.

Somehow she knew you would need her guidance."

Oliver nodded. He didn't actually agree, didn't think his grandmother had thought much about him one way or the other. He'd rarely seen her. But if it comforted his mother to think that, then so be it.

"Might I go up and fetch them?"

She reached for his hand and gave it a squeeze. "May they bring you a sense of commonality my poor mother never experienced. She seemed so solitary and alone in this world."

"What about Great-uncle Paul? Did they never talk together about their experiences?"

"Not to my knowledge. He was...very odd. The less said about him, the better." With that cryptic response, she rose and led the way upstairs. She left Oliver to mount the narrower steps to the small space under the eaves where keepsakes from their old house were stored. It wasn't a full attic, and he had to nearly crawl to the chest she'd described.

Inside was a stack of small books bound in cloth and leather. He opened one and beheld his grandmother's spidery, old-fashioned writing He'd never been much interested in learning about his crazy forebears, but now a fillip of excitement twisted inside him. What might he learn from these yellowed pages? What if he could develop his ability and become a medium in truth and not a fraud? Surely the fruits of his labor would be even more lucrative.

And of course, he'd be helping people.

Oliver made his crooked way back out of the crawlspace, carrying an awkward armful of the books. He did not wish to linger and visit with his mother now, so he thanked her for the journals, bid her good-bye and hurried back to his rooms with the booty.

For the next three hours, he was engrossed in

Grandmother Silver's mind. He skimmed passages about the minutia of running the house, hiring servants, paying bills, buying hats, visiting her few friends, and zeroed in on the bits about her psychic experiences.

"*Visited Mrs. Cawley today and one of my spells overcame me. I saw in her drawing room the spirit of a woman who had ended her life there perhaps generations before. I experienced the spirit's pain, relived for countless years, the broken heart that led her to drink poison, her distress and her desire to take back what she had done. I have become quite adept at hiding the results of my affliction but this time I found myself muttering, 'Too late. Too late,' much to my mortification.*

"*I went into a faint and had to be revived with smelling salts. It was a shameful display, and I'm quite certain Mrs. Cawley will never be in to receive my call again.*"

The more Oliver read, the more he realized that over the span of sixty years, his grandmother had grown no more able to control her "spells" than he could. She couldn't summon the spirits at will nor dispel them when they visited her. They came at odd times in unexpected places and made her life a misery. It confirmed what he'd suspected—that being near a person or place that had been part of the death experience was what triggered the spell. Damned Robert Court had been with his cousin. Oliver could hear the word echoing in his own head— the memory of a memory. *Robert, Robert.*

He slammed closed the third book, one representing an early part of her life, and sat back in his chair. Perhaps this was a door he did not want to open further. Not even to help Robert Court. The idea of being a real psychic no longer seemed appealing. Inventing stories and false messages was much better than suffering long-dead pain and coming away with a headache.

Oliver noticed the afternoon light was waning and checked his timepiece. It was far later than he'd expected, and he had an appointment across town this evening. Lady Markham's good friend Mrs. Veda Stull was having a small meeting at her house tonight. Oliver was the guest of honor, invited to explain Spiritualism to the uninitiated among the guests and then to give a display of his powers.

It was the last thing he wanted to do tonight. He'd had enough of otherworldly nonsense, both real and imaginary. He'd like nothing better than to forget it all, go to a pub and drink himself under the table with a cheerful crowd of strangers. No. What he'd like even more would be another bout with Robert Court. No talking about Lily and murder, only fierce, grunting, thrusting, violent sex between two willing men. But that wasn't likely to happen.

Oliver put the journals aside and went to prepare for the evening. He brushed his second-best suit—with all his new engagements, it was time for a trip to the tailor—and put on a fresh shirt, collar and tie.

He put on his coat and hat and walked around the corner to the pie shop, eating the greasy mutton pie carefully so he wouldn't spot his shirt. Then he started toward Veda Stull's house.

His route took him close to the site of Lily's murder, and as he drew nearer the street, he found his feet slowing and turning almost of their own accord to go revisit the place. He studied the houses and the nearby churchyard and considered where Lily might have been running to. Why had she been on this particular street so late in the evening? True, it wasn't far from her home, according to Court, but it wasn't as if there were shops she might've been visiting. Only houses.

So whom had she been visiting and why? Or had she been

returning home from someplace farther away? Would a woman like her be walking alone? It seemed whatever her errand had been that evening might shed some light on what had happened to her. Had the police even considered the possible circumstances before hanging a halfwit for the crime? It seemed Court had pursued other leads after they'd called the case solved. Oliver wondered what he'd learned.

A feeling of nausea washed through him, and his immediate thought was that the mutton pie wasn't sitting well. In fact, he thought he was about to lose it onto the pavement as his stomach churned. Then the sensations began... Lily's sensations, which were getting far too familiar. The dizziness and fear rushed through him, and it was all he could do to remain upright. Oliver hurried off the road and leaned against the nearest building as the flashes came faster. A dark hulking shape. Hard, grasping hands, and then, oh God, the pain in his head, and he was gasping for breath. For life.

*This is for the best, my dear.* Words sounded in his ear. He could hear them as clearly as if the man had spoken directly to him. That was something new.

Oliver rubbed his hands over his face and shook his head, trying to clear it. The gravestones in the fenced churchyard caught his attention, and he *remembered* seeing them as he fought for his life. Not him. Lily. Not his memories. Hers. Oliver's mind was all twisted up and confused, and he wanted to get out of here quickly.

He just didn't know if his legs would support him.

He pushed away from the brick wall and headed toward the church, gripping the fence to help him keep balance as he walked. He gazed through the bars and saw a gardener trimming the ivy that was starting to overtake a few of the headstones.

Oliver stopped walking and clung to the bars. "Pardon me," he called.

The man looked up, trimmers in one hand, ivy trailing from the other. "Yes, sir? Can I help you?"

"You've worked here for some time?"

"Not too long, sir. I just come down from the north some months ago. I'm replacin' the old gent that used to be the gardener."

"So you weren't here last year at this time? Didn't hear about the murder on Guy Fawkes Night?"

His head bobbed so hard, his cap nearly fell off. "Oh, aye, I *heard* about it, all right. Don't think anyone in the parish will ever forget that poor young woman being killed practically on the church doorstep. They still talk about it."

"But you weren't here, so you didn't witness anything."

"No, sir. Everybody said that dustman was a quiet, polite little man. Just did his job and never caused any trouble. Gives you chills thinking about the hidden darkness in some people, don't it?"

"Yes, that it does." Oliver started to walk on.

"If you don't mind my asking, why do you want to know?" the man called after him. "Are you a friend or a relative of that murdered girl's?"

"Something like that."

Maybe closer than either. Lily was a part of him now, embedded in his mind like a thorn or a sliver. They were linked, and he thought he couldn't completely rid himself of her until she rested peacefully. He paused for a moment to consider. Lord, he hoped she'd leave him then. He didn't wish to be inhabited by a ghost for the rest of his days.

## Chapter Seven

Oliver sat in the drawing room, eyes squeezed tight, trying not to think about Lily Bailey or even young Victoria Stull, dead from a fever these three years.

Mrs. Veda Stull, the dead girl's mother, was an attentive, kindly hostess. Another wealthy one, as well. He was offered tea and cakes—he was often treated like a guest rather than a tradesman, though he'd labeled himself a messenger from the other side.

Yet he refused the refreshments from the Stulls' excellent kitchen. And as he instructed the others on what he would do and what they might expect to see, he felt a twinge of guilt. He usually only indulged in such emotion late at night, alone in his rooms.

With grave faces and the rustle of starched cloth, they took their seats at the linen-covered table, set out exactly as he'd instructed. His hands felt as if they'd been immersed in ice water, and he was grateful that the lady next to him had warm fingers.

He knew that Mrs. Prendergast wanted to hear from her husband, and after the usual eyes rolling back, tremors and gasps, he managed a greeting from the late George to his beloved Augusta. But the slippery chill in his spine distracted him.

"Yes, yes." He gasped again as he pretended to be seized by the next spirit, Mrs. Stull's daughter, Victoria. "She is very happy in the next world. Your little Tory..." He stopped, horrified, because he felt the moisture slipping down his face. He was crying.

He needed to gain control of himself and stop. Immediately.

Rather than say another word, he feigned a swoon and managed to thump his head hard on the table in front of him. Ouch. His forehead bounced on the wood.

He turned his cheek to rest on the tablecloth but kept his eyes shut. The tears still slid down his cheeks. Tory, poor little Tory, he thought. The serious girl in the photograph was long gone, he expected. And so was Lily. It was all just echoes. He didn't move, waiting for the tears to stop, while the ladies and the one gentleman around the table called for burnt feathers, smelling salts, brandy.

Oliver allowed himself a full minute of simply breathing and relaxing before he opened his eyes to see all the concerned faces around him.

"You were wonderful," Mrs. Stull said as he sat up, feeling as groggy as he might if he'd actually fainted or fallen asleep. "I am so reassured."

He could only nod. It was beyond him to touch her hand and murmur the soothing false words he usually employed at this point of the proceedings. How could she be reassured? He'd given her nothing. Found...nothing. The howling went on inside him.

This new reality he'd stumbled over was raw and jagged. He wanted to return to the comfort of his old pretenses. But he didn't expect to be comfortable again, unless he could find Robert Court and demand he hold him. How odd that the catalyst of his horrible newfound skills, the very man who would probably throw him in prison, should offer the one refuge Oliver sought.

He straightened his tie, pulled out his handkerchief and wiped his face.

"Will you stay and have tea with us?" Mrs. Stull asked. The others, with their shiny, reverent faces, nodded and murmured their hopes that he would honor them with his presence.

*Christ, no.* The need to escape pressed in on him, the same sensation he'd felt in Lady Markham's rooms and during those few days he'd held a regular job. Perhaps the bothersome spirits had always been chasing him away from other people. He almost laughed aloud.

"I am most grateful," he managed to say as he fumbled his gloves from his pocket and pulled them on. He would have fled without payment if Mrs. Stull hadn't gently pressed the envelope into his hand. He usually asked for the "donations" beforehand, to keep him from being distracted, he explained to his hosts, and allow him to leave this plane of existence.

Mrs. Stull led him to the front door herself, trying to lend him the use of her carriage, pleading with him to come back and sit down, for he seemed far too wan. "You must still have one foot in the ethereal world," she said with a touch of wonder.

He refused as politely as possible and almost sprinted to the door. When he opened it, a familiar form stood on the doorstep, hand raised to the knocker.

Court didn't appear surprised to find him standing there, but Oliver felt a jolt of something akin to joy at the unexpected sight of the detective. The man hadn't warned him he'd be coming tonight.

Court looked past Oliver and removed his hat before nodding at their hostess. "Am I late, Mrs. Stull?"

"Oh, Mr. Peeler, I am so sorry. Lady Markham wasn't certain if you would be one of our guests today. Poor Mr. Marsh suffered a turn, so we had to cut short our communion with the other side. He insists on leaving. I wish I could make him take my carriage."

Court turned those cool gray eyes on Oliver. "He does seem rather pale. Have no fear, ma'am, I shall escort him home."

"There is no need," Oliver said like an idiot. *Please yes*, he thought. *Come back with me.*

Court rocked back on his heels and looked him up and down. "If you fainted, Mr. Marsh, I hardly think you should wander the streets alone."

Marsh wasn't about to protest any longer. He thanked his hostess again and walked slowly down the stairs.

They walked away while Mrs. Stull watched.

"I did not faint," Oliver said.

"Hmm. Pretended to, then?"

Mr. Court had seen him at his worst, or rather at his strangest, but still seemed unimpressed by the touch of the eerie in him. Such a firm comfort of a man, and suddenly Marsh felt almost lighthearted. "You will not trick me into admitting to trickery, Inspector."

"You are pale, though. Perhaps we should stop for a drink." God, now the gruff concern in Court's voice unsettled him. Oliver's emotions raced up and down—he hadn't felt such careening since he was a boy of fifteen.

"You do not need to coddle me. I am not a tender young girl," he growled.

"Girl, most definitely not. Tender and young, perhaps."

Oliver stopped walking. "What are you saying, Mr. Court?"

Court stood next to him and pushed his hands into his trouser pockets. "Perhaps you need a cup of tea instead of a stronger drink. I wouldn't want to have to carry you back to your lodgings, though strolling down the street with a man slung over my shoulder might be an interesting...novelty." He turned his gaze to a starling pecking at an apple core, but the corners of his mouth were ever so slightly tipped up, and Oliver knew he had not mistaken the matter. The solid Inspector Court was flirting with him.

His spirits rose once again, to giddying heights, and he continued walking, swiftly now. His steps slowed when he realized he must talk about Lily. He wanted to speak of the matter to Robert before he forgot what he'd sensed.

He waited until they'd passed the nurse pushing the perambulator with two charges in tow.

"Before I went to Mrs. Stull's house, I visited the spot where... The place where Lily died."

Court nodded as if to say go on.

"I am convinced that the man who did this is well-bred, or at least has the accents of someone well-bred, and I—or rather she—knew him. He was no doltish dustman."

"You heard him?"

Oliver nodded. "He had a pleasant, worried tone, almost"— he cleared his throat— "almost loving. A tenor, I think. Not young, not old." He pressed his fingers to his temple, which throbbed. "He knew her. The way he spoke, the way she saw him had...had changed. He seemed large, looming. Oh, God." Oliver stopped again, and Court was right there, a hand on his arm, steadying, grounding him to life.

Oliver swallowed the nausea. "How big is...was Lily? How tall, I mean? Though, wait, I, we, were on the ground then. So I'm not sure if that is what I saw." He knew he babbled, but Court apparently understood.

"She stood only to your shoulder, perhaps five-three."

"Maybe that's why he seemed so big. He may not have been

even as tall as I."

"Good. That's good. Take your time to think. Maybe you'll recall more detail," Court said, and Oliver imagined him speaking to frightened witnesses with that encouraging warmth.

Oliver shook his head, which created another wave of nausea. He put his hand over his mouth. "I need to stop thinking about it. Not forever, but I feel as if it is devouring me."

"Ah, no, indeed. We can't have that," Court said. "No one else may devour you."

God above, the man had shifted into outright suggestiveness. Oliver laughed.

"That's the ticket." Court pulled out a watch and peered down at it. Perhaps someday he'd require glasses. Wire rims would add a note of the scholar and make him even more appealing. "I insist that we stop for a meal, Mr. Marsh. I shall pay."

"You needn't order me about as if I was a patrol officer under you."

"You'd be a sergeant. And at the moment, I'm not working with anyone else. Only you. Under me."

Oliver rolled his eyes but felt his ears burn. And predictably, his cock twitched as he imagined the outrageous possibilities. The statements coming from Court's mouth might have sounded greasy or bizarre, but he spoke in that grave, calm policeman's manner, without a hint of the winking suggestiveness—which made the words even more heat-inducing.

Court had never in his life spoken in such a lewd manner, but he already knew Marsh well enough to understand that the man loved to laugh—even more than most people.

The sickly green cast to his face, those heavy bags under those expressive eyes, had worried Court, and made him want to drag Marsh to a Harley Street doctor. Marsh wouldn't agree, so he changed his plans. He'd jolly the man into relaxing, bully him into eating, and then... Well. He was arousing himself with the lewd remarks he was making. How odd to learn that he had a propensity for bawdy nonsense—and that it affected him. The effort to make Marsh relax and laugh was creating some trouble for himself.

But even as he murmured suggestive phrases to the man who gasped with feigned outrage and real arousal, Court was preoccupied with making lists of the men he knew and who'd known Lily. Men with tenor, well-bred voices. That included Marsh, of course, but thank the good Lord for that alibi—he was not on the list of suspects. Not of that crime, at any rate.

Court huffed a small breath of contempt. He wasn't going to collar Marsh for bilking his customers. Couldn't stand to do it now, but the trouble was, he had no other excuse to stay near the medium, unless Marsh could reveal the names of other swindlers, and Court doubted he would.

If he must, Court would take time off from the force. It wouldn't be the best possible move for his career—even a request of a week's leave would make Hardy extremely unhappy. And should he discover Court used the time to burrow into a closed case, especially *that* particular case, the superintendent would grow livid. But Court discovered he cared more about finding the truth of Lily's death than his own advancement.

He shoved his hands in his pockets again and looked sideways at Marsh. Yes, all right, there were other reasons he wanted to take the time away from his work.

They walked some time before they encountered a decent-looking public house, and by then, Marsh's appearance had improved and his hands no longer shook.

They ordered two pints and a plate of bread, cold meats and cheese and sat at a rickety table near the door.

Marsh drew in a long breath as if he loved the acrid scent of old beer and smoke.

"Thank you." He lifted his pint and used it to salute Court.

"You need to eat, as well," Court reminded him. "You fainted at Mrs. Stull's."

"I truly did not faint. It's not any easier when the sensation hits, but I think the recovery from the experience doesn't take as long. No bleeding this time." He paused, glass partway to his mouth. "Oh, and no blurting out unfortunate phrases."

He took a long drink, and the pale foam remained on his top lip until he licked it off. He grinned at Court, who looked away.

Out on the street, as they walked together, Court could make the teasing remarks about... Christ, about doing obscene things to this man. But face-to-face in the small quiet pub, he suddenly felt a touch of confusion when their eyes met. As his own sexual excitement increased, he grew less willing to express it. And there was the simple and dreary matter of being found out. What if someone should see the looks they exchanged?

He stared into his pint of lager and tried to think of something to say that wouldn't remind either of them of their nude bodies slippery with the sweat created by that mouthwatering exercise.

Marsh ate a bit of cheese. "I expect you'll want to talk to the men, or rather the gentlemen, who knew Lily and match the description I gave you."

Court sighed. Yes, that would certainly do the trick of depleting sexual tension. "I'd like to, and I shall, but I mustn't draw attention to the fact that I'm looking into Lily's death. I have to be discreet."

"But you must do something! You cannot ignore the fact that the wrong man hanged for her death." Marsh broke off a piece of bread but didn't eat it. Instead, he crumbled it between his long fingers; all the while, he stared, without blinking once, down at his hands without apparently seeing their movement.

This behavior seemed odder than any he'd exhibited when he'd been struck by the strange visions. At last Marsh looked up. "He's done it before. I don't know why we—I mean why I know this. Why she knows it or how I feel it. But listen to me, Robert Court." He leaned across the table. "You must do something. I'm nearly certain that Lily is not the only one."

He popped the remaining crumb of bread into his mouth and washed it down with the last of his beer. "If you don't do something about that man, I will. Even if Lily was the only victim, she deserves better."

Court held up his hands in a gesture of surrender. "Yes, yes, I know. I have been working at finding the killer since the day she died. But it will do me no good if someone alerts the superintendent that I am once again poking my nose into this business. I will lose my job just as certainly as we are sitting here if so much as a hint of my activity reaches him. I'm not giving up. I'm merely saying I have to be careful. It will be easy enough for me to talk with my family members, but she also met a great number of people through her fiancé, Phillip."

"Could he be the guilty party?"

Court shook his head. "He was almost as far away from the scene as you were. And he was entirely undone by her death. The poor man still mourns." Excessively, perhaps. Was that a symptom of guilt? Court thought of something else. "Also he has a rich deep baritone, not a tenor."

"So you believe me." Marsh sat back in his chair and looked as pleased as if he'd been given a great sum of money.

"I do, to an extent."

"What does that mean?"

"He could have disguised his voice. She could have been fatally struck at the moment and her hearing failed. It might be another memory from another time. From another person, perhaps."

"Oh. You're right, I suppose. But you believe that I am not lying."

Court nodded. "I do believe you."

"Thank you," Marsh said softly. "Hearing that is good. It matters a great deal to me." He half closed his eyes and made a soft humming sound of concentration. "If her fiancé is that sorrowful, perhaps someone might recommend a medium to him. And whoever speaks to Phillip should mention that as many people as possible who knew her should attend the séance. Some hogwash about a strong masculine atmosphere would help ease her fear. Yes, that would do the trick. Bring the gentlemen from her life to help guide her troubled spirit to speak to me. The helpful medium."

Court should have been outraged at hearing the deception planned to dupe members of the public. He was only intrigued. But then he shook his head. "Marsh, this isn't your battle. It has nothing to do with you."

"The devil it doesn't." Marsh gave an unamused chuckle. "Haven't you been listening? Her death is lodged inside me like a broken-off spear. Lily's battle became mine since that day at Lady Markham's house." Now he smiled more broadly. "I think my work for her is rewarded, however."

"What do you mean?" Court picked up his glass and finished off his beer. "You won't get much money from Phillip's family. They aren't like Markham or Stull."

"Not money, Mr. Court. You. I have decided that Lily's reward to me is you."

# Chapter Eight

Once more Oliver followed the inspector up the steps to his flat, as excited as a lad going to a country fair, knowing he'd have candy floss and a good long ride on a roundabout. What a thrill, and there was no wondering about what would happen between them this time. Although Court hadn't said anything in response to Oliver's comment about him being a reward, soon after that, he'd paid the bill and led the way from the pub, clearly as anxious as Oliver to get someplace private.

They'd walked quickly in the direction of Oliver's place, and he fit the key to the lock, threw the door open, and they hurried inside. Before Oliver could even close the door behind them, Court grabbed him roughly by the arms and drew him close, seizing his mouth in a hard kiss. Oliver gave a little *mmph* of surprise as soft lips mashed against his and a warm tongue insinuated between them. He grasped Court's coat and clung to it while the other man's arms slid around him and held him tight. *This* was what he'd been longing for, a powerful embrace from the solid man. It made him feel safe and grounded in the world, as if nothing truly awful could happen to him so long as Court was with him.

After a few moments of fervent exploration, Court released his mouth and pulled back to gaze into his eyes. "This what you wanted?"

"Yes," Oliver gasped.

"And this?" Court unbuttoned Oliver's coat and pushed it

off his arms, then set to work on the rest of Oliver's buttons—jacket, waistcoat, shirt. There were far too many buttons. In a fit of impatience, Court popped off a few in his efforts to get Oliver shirtless. He stripped him of undershirt, trousers, drawers, garters and socks and shoes. All of it quickly dispensed with until Oliver stood completely nude before him.

Court, meanwhile, had not taken off so much as his coat.

Oliver trembled with lust and anticipation. There was something extremely erotic about being absolutely nude and exposed in front of the fully clothed Court.

"Turn around and place your hands against the door." The man's voice was as rough as gravel, and his eyes glittered eerily in the gaslight.

Heat flared in Oliver's groin as he obeyed, pressing palms against smooth wood and peeling paint. He leaned forward so his legs were slightly behind him.

"Spread your legs wider," Court growled.

Oliver shuffled his feet farther apart. His buttocks tensed, and his anus tightened. The tip of his erect cock brushed against the door before him. He stood, awaiting the next instruction, but silence followed. He imagined Court's eyes examining him, dwelling on his backside. The touch of that gaze was like hot wax drizzling all over his body. He gritted his teeth and waited, listened to the slow approach of Court's footsteps, then felt a light touch on one inner thigh.

His asshole was clenching and opening spasmodically now, yearning for something to enter it. Oliver shivered as Court's warm, ungloved fingers brushed up and down his thighs as light as the touch of a feather. Just that. No more. And then the hands moved to touch his back, stroking lightly from shoulders to hip. Gooseflesh rose on his skin. The muscles of his rear tightened more; his cock was rock hard with desire.

And still Court teased him. He rested his hands on Oliver's shoulders and smoothed them down his arms to his wrists while his body pressed close. Oliver glanced at the blunt-fingered hands gripping his wrists, felt the layers of clothing tickling his backside and the warmth of the body pressed against him. He held his breath and listened to Court breathing near his ear. Did the man seek some sort of response, or was Oliver meant to submit in silence?

"Do you... Would you like me to suck you...sir?" he asked hesitantly, inserting the formal address in an erotic context.

"If I wanted you to, I'd already have you down on your knees," Court growled. "Hush and do exactly as I bid you, when I bid you."

He shuddered at the rude treatment, wanted more of those controlling words taking away his power and telling him exactly how to perform.

Court rocked gently against him. Even through layers of cloth, Oliver could feel his hardness. Then abruptly he stepped away. Oliver shifted, regaining his balance after the loss of that weight against him, and he turned his head to glance over his shoulder.

An unexpected slap across his buttocks shook him. "Did I tell you to move? Face down. Eyes on the floor."

Oliver smiled and obeyed. Of course, when he looked down, what he saw was his raging erection, looking as if it would drill a hole into the door it pressed against. With every fiber of his being, he wanted Court to reach around his hip and grasp his cock, but instead the detective resumed lighter touches. This time it was his lips rather than his fingers that caressed Oliver's back, delicious, soft, warm kisses trailing down his spine.

Christ, where had this down-to-earth man learned to play such erotic games? Oliver would've pegged him for the type who went in for quick, furtive fucks in a dark alley and then slinking off into the night—no finesse or care taken. But his technique was amazing.

Court spread Oliver's buttocks apart and traced a dampened finger down the cleft, circling his opening before probing just a fingertip inside the constricting ring of muscle. Oliver groaned and pushed back against the finger. This earned another hard slap from Court across one cheek.

"Don't wiggle."

"No, sir," Oliver answered promptly as a soldier responding to his commanding officer.

"Or release, no matter how much you might want to."

"Wouldn't dream of it." But his cock was aching and already beaded with fluid at the tip. He bumped his cockhead against the door, seeking the slightest bit of relief.

Court returned to kissing him, lower on his back now and across the swell of his buttocks. The little kisses soothed the tingling in his skin from the smacks but stoked the raging need in his groin. He needed more, so much more than gentle kisses and touches.

By the time Court finally slid one hand between his legs to cradle his balls, Oliver was trembling and sweating. And then, oh blessed relief, the other man moved his hand higher and gripped Oliver's cock. Lightly, he smoothed his fist up its length, drawing the foreskin over the head, then down again.

Oliver stared down at the disembodied hand rubbing his cock. It was a beautiful sight, the strong fist gliding up and down his shaft, alternately revealing and concealing his cockhead. He couldn't resist rocking his hips just a little and earned a stern, "Steady on or you'll get another smacking," from Court.

It was an impossible request, of course. How could a man

resist thrusting when such wonderful sensations coursed through him? Court's warm palm gliding over his skin was quickly moving him toward ecstasy. And then the man draped himself over Oliver's back again like the world's heaviest cloak. He wrapped Oliver in his embrace, pulling him away from the door and enfolding him in his arms. Lips skated over the edge of Oliver's jaw, bestowing sweet, damp kisses.

"Now to your bed," he whispered and guided Oliver toward the other room.

They walked like that, so close together they might have been one being with four legs. Awkward but lovely. Oliver smiled as they stumbled through the door frame and into his small room.

The bed was unmade from last night's sleep, and Court pushed Oliver back onto the rumpled sheets. Oliver lay on his back, silent, waiting, watching as his handsome suitor took his time untying his tie, opening his collar, removing each article of clothing.

The other man's gaze was predatory, assessing Oliver in a hungry way that made his stomach catapult. Still, Court unfastened each cufflink with utmost care and set them on the nightstand. Each slow movement was designed to be casual and to torment the waiting Oliver. But he could see the ruse wasn't easy for Court either. His breathing was shallow, and the bulge in his trousers was telltale. Underneath that cool exterior, it was clear the man wanted to leap onto the bed and attack Oliver, toy with him like a lion with prey.

Mmm, Oliver wanted him to do just that, tear into him with teeth and hard, demanding hands. Oliver reclined with his arms folded behind his head, nonchalant, as if he weren't squirming with need. He rocked his hips a little, thrusting his jutting cock into the air, and gazed right back at Robert Court, a heavy-lidded look meant to entice the other man to mount him with utmost haste.

As he removed his braces and undershirt, Court gave a little groan or growl, some kind of rumbling sound that sent a fresh wave of lust rushing through Oliver. Ah, anticipation, maybe the best part of the mating game. But this play had gone on long enough, and now he was ready for much more.

At last Court finished removing his last article of clothing, but even then he stood for a moment in naked, powerful perfection, watching Oliver. Maybe he wanted a sign, some indication—in case a raging erection wasn't sufficient—that Oliver was aroused by the sight of him. Very well. Oliver swept his gaze over the other man, slowly, head to toe. He let his tongue slick his lips, swallowed, and raised his knees so his pelvis was tilted up. Could he be more inviting than that? *Come, fuck me*, he begged with his eyes.

Court moved toward the bed with a measured tread. He climbed onto the mattress, which sagged, and the metal frame squealed in protest at the additional weight.

"There's ointment for lubrication in the nightstand," Oliver murmured.

Court glanced that direction but made no move to get it. "Not yet. We will do something else tonight."

He felt a momentary stab of frustration. He felt primed for entry, wanted Court to thrust into him. But his disappointment was quickly supplanted by pleasure as Court crawled on top of him, positioning his body in the opposite direction. His knees bracketed Oliver's shoulders, cock and balls flopping against his chin. Court's hairy stomach tickled his chest, and his hands and mouth were soon occupied in delightful spots below Oliver's waist. Unexpectedly inventive, Court was a treasure chest of surprises.

Oliver nuzzled the man's ball sac, soft against his mouth, licked it and inhaled the musky fragrance before burrowing his head lower, seeking his cock. He had to reach his hand between them to position the head at his lips; then he sucked it in bit by bit, earning a contented grunt from Court. Both the scent and salty taste of the other man permeated his senses.

Meanwhile, down below, the remarkable wetness of Court's mouth gobbled his cock. The ache in Oliver's balls eased a little as wonderful heat surrounded him. He whimpered around the thick flesh filling his throat and lifted his hips to get even more of that warmth around him. A gagging sound came from Court, and then a sharp slap snapped across Oliver's balls. He jerked and yelped around his mouthful of cock.

"Settle, boy," Court ordered and pinned Oliver's hips to the bed to keep him from thrusting again.

Oliver mentally chuckled at the discipline, then turned his attention to giving Court as much pleasure as the man was bestowing on him. He gripped Court's buttocks and tilted his head back, making a better angle for Court to fuck his throat. The big cock filled him near to choking before receding as Court pulled away. In and out, the other man pumped.

Oliver closed his eyes and imagined himself a receptacle for Court's pleasure—submissive and open to please his...master. The thought sent waves of excitement coursing through him. He was thrilled by the subservient role, which came as naturally to him as breathing. Always had. He never took the top position during sex and enjoyed a controlling, dominating man in his bed.

Court might be on top, pinning Oliver down and holding him exactly as he wished, but the man was generous with the pleasure he offered as well. Saliva lubricated the glide of Oliver's cock in Court's mouth, a warm, lovely feeling like honey coating him. The man's teeth scraped Oliver's shaft as he withdrew; then Court grabbed it in a vise grip and pumped with his fist while bobbing the tip in and out of his mouth. No more gagging for Mr. Court. His top position afforded him the option of nearly choking Oliver with his increasingly deep thrusts, while controlling how far Oliver's cock might enter his throat.

And that was fine. Oliver bent his head at in impossible angle, seeking to take as much length as the dominant man would give him. He was a good boy, a willing boy, eager to earn the headmaster's praise for his efforts. Such images flashed in his mind as the pressure in his balls wound tighter and tighter and then exploded through him. He groaned as his spending poured through him and into Court's mouth. A soft gulping sound floated from below as the man swallowed.

The heavy body on top of him was shuddering now, Court's arse flexing beneath his hands. Oh, he was close. Oliver could feel the desperate need trembling in him and knew exactly what the other man was feeling, poised on the cusp of something, waiting for a final nudge to push him over the edge. How splendid and wonderful to be able to give that nudge to him. Oliver squeezed his eyes closed, tears leaking from the corners at his efforts not to gag, and he accepted the benediction of Court's cock as it released into his throat. He swallowed, happy to receive what his lover gave.

Lover? Was that what Robert Court was to him now? They'd had two encounters, which was one more than Oliver had had with anybody since Maurice in France. After those heavenly days and their bitter aftermath, he'd settled on becoming just another London firefly, drifting from one encounter to another with none of them meaning anything more than an instant's pleasure. Firefly was his own term for it because of that brief flash of bliss before darkness resumed.

But with Court... God, he would happily have the man in

his bed every night. What was it about the solemn, straight-and-narrow man that lit him up so?

Court withdrew from his mouth, wet cock flopping heavily against Oliver's face. Oliver exhaled a deep breath and rubbed his cheek against the warmth of the other man's groin. He wanted to coat himself in the scent and keep it on him after Court was gone. Or to be marked as the man's possession in some more permanent way.

His reaction frightened him. He was falling hard and fast for someone as different from Maurice as the sun was from the moon. Only the two men's dominant tendencies were the same. But Court would never consider forging a relationship such as Oliver had shared with Maurice, however briefly. Court was an upright citizen who just happened to have a secret side, but he would not hold Oliver in deepest affection and care for him in that way.

Oliver squirmed beneath the hot, heavy body pinning him down. He had to get free of Court so he could breathe, and he must never let the other man guess the unruly feelings he was entertaining. It would not do at all.

Robert Court rolled to the side, releasing Oliver at last. They lay on their sides for a moment that way, facing each other in opposition. The bed was so narrow, Oliver could feel his rear jutting over the edge of it. A wonder they hadn't collapsed the poor old piece of furniture.

"That was something different," Oliver said to fill the silence, but his light tone belied the heavier emotions roiling around in his gut. He reached out and rested a hand on Court's ankle, feeling solid tissue and bone. "Perhaps you've had more experience than I'd imagined."

Court lifted an eyebrow. "You've imagined how much experience I may or may not have?"

"I've spent a good deal of time thinking about you since we met. Hard not to dwell on a man who intends to ruin my livelihood. How did you become an inspector?"

The other man shook his head. "I don't believe we must share our histories."

"Why not? I'm sure your investigation has revealed much about me and my background. Why shouldn't I at least know a little about you?"

"Because it isn't pertinent in solving Lily's murder. You don't require my personal story."

"Neither are sexual relations pertinent, yet we indulged in those. Twice. Is there some great secret about your choosing to enter police work that you don't wish to share?"

Court paused, then rubbed his finger over his upper lip absently as if stroking a moustache. Oliver imagined he might've shaved one off not too long before.

"Very well. It's a simple enough story. My grandfather was a bricklayer, but my father, through hard work and perseverance, became a tradesman, a well-respected, solid citizen in the building industry. His ambition to provide lasting financial stability for our family inspired him to invest as well, which would have been all right if he'd stuck to treasury bonds or some such, but he gave a great deal of money to the wrong person. A confidence man enticed him to part with most of the security he'd spent a lifetime accumulating. He was devastated when he realized he'd been fooled. It broke his spirit and, I believe, brought on early death."

Court stared at him until Oliver couldn't bear to hold the other man's gaze any longer. He looked at the ankle he was still petting, studied the fine brown hair on Court's calf. "I see. Thus your desire to expose fraud."

"Among other things. I believe in justice and the law and

have devoted my life to them. It is as much of a calling as the priesthood."

"A noble pursuit," Oliver said and wondered how Court justified mixing with a man who hoaxed people on a regular basis. He must despise Oliver even while he enjoyed fucking him.

*This will not end well. You do know that,* his inner voice calmly informed him. *You've begun to crave this upright man too much, but he will never give himself to you as fully as you wish. And very likely, he'll see you behind bars before this is over.*

A heavy hand settled on Oliver's leg, drawing his attention back to Court's face. "I've told you a bit about me. Now I beg a return of the favor. What really brought you to Spiritualism and communing with the dead? Not that tale you tell your clients but the real truth. What convinced you to start bilking people and telling them lies?"

# Chapter Nine

The moment he'd spoken the words, Court wished them back. Although his assessment was true, it wasn't completely accurate, and Marsh frowned and flinched as if he'd been struck a blow. Now, in the aftermath of the most amazing sexual encounter Court had ever had, was not the time to attack the medium's fraudulent claims. Maybe later, when the man was clothed and less vulnerable.

But why should it matter? Oliver Marsh had taken advantage of people during their most vulnerable time of mourning. He *was* a liar and a cheat—except where his experience with Lily was concerned—and he did deserve to be called out on it. He should be able to accept the truth about himself. Court needn't worry about sparing his feelings.

It was just the timing. Warm and glowing in the aftermath of their coupling, pressed close together on this narrow bed, it seemed wrong to attack. Court wanted to preserve the illusion that they were two men who had anything at all in common for just a bit longer.

"I apologize for the stern tone," he said. "I promise I shan't use your words against you, but I truly want to know what brought you to seek this livelihood."

Marsh lifted and dropped one shoulder. "It chose me, I suppose. Like you, I had a father who pursued bad investments—except mine also had a fondness for gaming tables. Only after he died did I learn the extent of his debt. I had to sell my mother's home and move her into more affordable accommodations. Creditors were hounding, and I needed to raise money quickly."

He slid his hand up Court's leg to the knee and back down to the ankle. Up, down, in slow, easy strokes that incredibly made Court's cock begin to twitch again.

"I had yet to work at a job since I'd been attending university—blissfully ignorant of the state of the family finances. After Father died, I immediately left my studies and tried to find any work I could to stave off the creditors. I worked as a clerk at a shipping company. The pay was low, and I could see years stretching out before me of mind-numbing minutia, sitting on a stool in a cold, cramped room. It would take so long to crawl out from under the weight of Father's debt and finally begin to live a life of my own."

Court nodded, sympathizing with that feeling of despair when a man realizes he must bear the burden of his father's mistakes. "And how did you decide to do what you do?"

"I changed jobs, tried to work in the livelier environment of the trading floor but was not able to overcome my inability to be in the midst of a crowd. This sounds like an excuse, I know, but I tend to lose breath and pass out in an extremely crowded or stuffy, confined room. At that point, I wanted only to escape. I met a man who invited me to travel to France with him. I left my mother as financially secure as I could and spent three lovely months abroad before the situation deteriorated."

Oliver glanced up at him. "I sound like the worst sort of selfish cad, don't I? Leaving my poor mother to pay the piper and running off with a lover. I can only say that I lost my senses. At any rate, I returned to England more destitute than before, saw an advertisement for a mentalist's performance in the newspaper, and the idea spoke to me. I knew I could do this—provide comfort to those in mourning. For a fee."

"Lying to the distraught is bad enough, but it's the fee that the law takes issue with, Marsh. I do as well. You must know in some part of yourself that what you're doing is wrong."

"Is it? I give real comfort to these people. They pay me to tell them what they crave to hear. And I must meet my expenses like anyone, so why should I not be paid for my service as you would be paid for locking up criminals?"

Court sat up, bracing a hand on Marsh's hip and perching on the edge of the narrow bed. "The difference is you're being paid for a service you aren't actually performing. You *can't* commune with the dead, can you? Except for this aberration with Lily."

"Perhaps I can. My grandmother and one of my uncles had a gift. Today I visited my mother, and she gave me Grandmother's journals. I hope to find aid within their pages to help me to develop this newfound psychic ability."

Those guileless blue eyes gazing up at him melted Court's resolve to teach some sort of lesson. Oliver Marsh was a fey creature who truly did seem to bring comfort to many people, all of whom were wealthy enough to afford him, so he was doing no real harm. Surely not enough to be thrown in prison. Besides, Court had already decided he couldn't bear to punish the man who'd given him a new lead in Lily's murder—and sexual joy such as he'd never experienced before.

He couldn't hurt Marsh, but what was he to do with him? He needed time to think without that beautiful body and those mesmerizing eyes draining him of his willpower.

He rose, reluctantly leaving the warmth of the bed and Marsh's body. "I must go. I cannot stay here another night. But I will see you again tomorrow, and I will arrange some sort of meeting with Mr. Phillip Hasel, my cousin's fiancé."

Oliver sat, arms clasped around his knees, tousled hair falling almost to his shoulders. "You can't remain even for a little while? It's early yet. I could pour us some tea. Or brandy."

"If I start sipping your brandy again, I may never make it home. No thank you." Court smiled, then impulsively stooped and grasped the back of Marsh's neck and kissed him soundly. "Good night."

He dressed quickly in the clothes he'd so recently provocatively shed and hurried from the room before the invisible cord tying him to Marsh drew him back into bed.

The things he'd done tonight tumbled through his mind, actions that were so unlike him it was as if he'd been possessed. The sexual position he'd suggested was one he'd read about in erotic literature, but he'd never imagined actually trying it. Tonight, all things had seemed possible. It was a night he would remember for the rest of his life, long after he was forced to bid good-bye to Oliver Marsh for the last time.

He told the superintendent he needed three days off. Hardy gave him the standard chin-tucked-stare-down-the-nose he used to intimidate the men on his staff, but Court gazed back without flinching. "I shan't draw a pay-packet during that time, I understand, sir. But the office is quiet for a change, and I'm going to use some of my time to finish the investigation into that medium Lord Markham complained of."

Hardy perked up. "That is good, Court. His lordship will be most pleased if we could at least warn the devil off. His wife's enthralled with the man."

Not exactly work for the criminal division, Court thought, but perhaps with the Marsh business wrapped up, he'd be back in Hardy's good graces, and he'd be given more interesting assignments. The Marsh business did interest him in some respects. Just that name brought the flutter of arousal.

Wilford, the sergeant he usually worked with, had been drafted to take part of the larger investigation into smuggling. Their paths didn't cross often lately, but Wilford stood near Court's desk, his large dirty hands clutching a mug of tea. He wore his full disguise of a dockworker. Bulky, with badly cut dark hair and a several-times broken nose, Wilford was a convincing navvy. Court wrinkled his nose. The sergeant even smelled the part.

"I'm glad to see you, sir." Wilford put down the mug. He lowered his voice. "I'm here just for that—to see you, I mean."

"And not the delicious, stewed tea?"

Wilford smiled, showing several gaps in his teeth. "The super had me into his office the other day asking if I wanted to work with another inspector permanently."

Blast. Maybe Court's hopes of returning to his former status were fantasy. "What did you say?"

"I told him no thank you. I said that Mr. Court might be a bit of a bulldog when it comes to working on a case, but that I thought your methods work."

Wilford wasn't a toady, so Court was pleasantly surprised to hear the praise. "Thanks," he said gruffly.

"But it made me wonder, sir, if there was something going on I wasn't privy to?" He meant politics, of course.

Court considered brushing aside the question. That would serve in keeping Wilford impressed by his authority. But Court had lately lost his patience with the hierarchy and the rules. "If there is, I'm not in on the secret either, sorry to say. You might be better served by saying yes, you'd rather work with another inspector."

Wilford wrinkled his slightly crooked nose and shook his head. "No, I'm not such a climber, sir."

Court was touched. His own ambition suddenly seemed silly, and he wondered if Wilford was the better man. He bid him good-bye and agreed that a nice murder would be just the thing to cheer them both up—and help Wilford lose a stone or two, an old joke the sergeant told to keep the others from mocking him. He was a tough copper, yet the poor man inevitably became sick after examining the scene of a murder. Wilford had even taken to carrying a bucket when responding to a call out to a murder scene.

Court wondered what Wilford would think of Marsh. Perhaps the day would come when their paths would cross. He imagined Marsh, head cocked to the side, solemnly listening to Wilford's descriptions of the pains he always felt in various parts of his body. Marsh was good at listening—the best confidence tricksters were.

Before he set out for Phillip's house, Court fetched Jock, who could use the exercise. Phillip liked the dog, and it would make his visit seem more like a social call rather than an investigation if Court brought Jock along.

The animal flung itself in happy circles around Court's feet and he had to tread carefully not to trip over it as they walked. After allowing Jock a few minutes of joyful celebration, Court called the dog to heel and attached the leash. He summoned a hack and, hauling a squirming Jock up under his arm, gave the driver the address to Phillip's house.

Jock panted happily at the window, growling at horses and dogs. Court tried to think of ways to introduce the topic of Marsh-the-Medium to his cousin's fiancé. He didn't want Phillip to gain some hope and actually believe Marsh might be able to speak to their lost Lily. Curse Marsh for seeming so reasonable in person yet so ridiculous when they were apart.

He sighed and patted Jock, who was snarling doggy obscenities at a passing milk-wagon.

The Hasel's butler greeted him—with a cultured, tenor voice, Court noticed—then stared off into space when Court didn't move for a few moments, giving him the opportunity to look the man up and down. About Marsh's height too.

"All right," he said.

The butler didn't ask him what he meant, only murmured, "This way, sir." And led him to Phillip, who sprang up from his seat in the slightly shabby bachelor's sitting room.

Phillip was delighted to see him, and Court felt another jab of guilt for not visiting more often.

He wasn't the only one feeling remorse. Phillip shook hands and said, "I should have been to see you, but your resemblance to my sweet Lily makes it difficult." He looked away. "I'm so sorry that I've been oversensitive."

"Hardly that. Never mind," Court said heartily. "I'm here now."

"Sit. Tell me about your cases." Phillip moved to the tray where a decanter sat. He poured them each a glass of something amber and handed one to Court, who selected a chair by the empty grate.

This was the opportunity, Court realized as he leaned down to stroke Jock's head. No need to venture far from the truth, though perhaps a bit of omission would be called for.

"I have been after a Spiritualist," he said. "One of those fraudulent swindlers who go after the bereaved. Except this one, this gentleman"—he grimaced—"I think he's not entirely a cheat."

Bother, he sounded pathetic.

Phillip downed his drink and poured another. "Do you think he actually can reach the other side?" he asked after a long minute. "If you were any other man, Court, I'd laugh and dismiss the notion at once. But you..." Leaning against the sideboard, he picked up the glass but didn't drink. His collar was crooked, he was too thin—the waistcoat and jacket he wore hung loose on him.

Court decided not to lie. "No. That is to say, I'm not sure what it is he hears or sees, but I have watched him, and I believe he sensed something. And it had to do with Lily." He took a tiny sip of the drink. Whiskey, single malt. "I don't discount wishful thinking on my part. There may be some of that involved, yes. But I came here because I hope to do a test."

"What is that?"

"It has to do with Mr. Marsh and his skill, of course. I wonder if you might arrange a meeting at your house."

"But you don't believe he's a true medium."

"He's something." Court suppressed a smile. "I don't want to give you too many details, but I hope you might invite all of the gentlemen older than twenty but under the age of fifty to whom you introduced Lily. I don't believe it needs to be a proper séance."

Phillip's eyes widened. "You think one of them killed her."

"The only thing I'm reasonably certain of is that the dustman who hanged was not the culprit."

Phillip groaned. "I want to go on with my life, Robert. I need to. Don't you understand?"

"Yes, I do. And I apologize for this imposition." He kept his voice gentle, but the way Phillip protested made the skin at the back of his neck prickle. And the fact that he'd avoided Court... Phillip Hasel had not murdered his fiancée, but could he have arranged the killing? Why would he have?

Phillip gave a wan smile. "No, no. I apologize for my outburst. I'm just finding life dreary. Of course I want to know the truth. If you believe that poor, moronic dustman was mistakenly hanged, how awful. I'll make a list of every man of a certain age who crossed paths with Lily. And please, there is no need to explain more to me. I'll invent some sort of inducement to have them come to my house."

Court nodded. "I shall foot any expenses. This event might prove to be nothing more than a congenial gathering."

"Will you wait while I write the names?"

"Yes, please. And thank you, Phillip. You should issue the invitation, but may I have a copy of that list?" He'd take the list and compare it to the notes he'd made based on the chatty letters he'd received from her and his own jotted-down memories of Lily's conversations.

Phillip seated himself at the table when the manservant entered the room. "The curate is here to collect the articles for the white elephant sale."

Phillip looked up, aggrieved. "Oh, bother. I forgot all about that. My mother should have taken care of the matter but is away. Send him in and allow me to make my apologies."

Thomas Patterson, the curate, was a round-faced gentleman more advanced in age than most men in his position. "How do you do, sir," he said as he shook Court's hand. "You have a familiar appearance. Have we met?"

"Perhaps you met my cousin, the late Lily Bailey."

The curate paled slightly and stammered. "Yes, yes, that must be it. I'm so sorry for your loss, sir." He was obviously new at his work. Most clergymen would be far more fluent in the face of mourning relations.

"Did you know my cousin well, Mr. Patterson?" Court asked.

"She came to services at my church several times, but I have only lately arrived at this parish." He gave a little laugh. "I am rather old to be starting with this career."

That explained the awkwardness. Or perhaps the man was always ill at ease, because he seemed unable to hold still. Mr. Patterson reached down and stroked Jock, who licked his hand. "Such a nice dog," he said. "I'll be on my way. The vicar sends kindest regards, Mr. Hasel, and hopes to see you on Sunday, as do I."

Court said, "We were just organizing a little party. I do hope you'll attend. I'll be sure to ask Phillip to send you an invitation."

The curate beamed. "It would be a great honor. Thank you." He bowed and left.

"Why did you invite him?" Phillip grumbled. "He's the most straitlaced, prosy fool I've ever met. If you want the men in attendance to speak freely, they won't with him around."

Court didn't think anyone needed to speak to Marsh for his unreliable skills to work. He imagined a room full of men and Marsh shaking hands with each—until he fell into some kind of trance. The spasms or whatever he felt were so painful to watch, a part of him hoped Marsh would spend the evening merely talking, laughing—and feeling nothing stronger than the dizziness of too much drink. But that was only a passing emotion. Court wanted Lily's killer more than he wanted Marsh's comfort. He'd only feel temporary discomfort, he reminded himself.

Phillip sat at the writing table, scratching down names, pausing, writing some more. Court stood by and occasionally reminded him of other places he might have taken Lily and introduced her to gentlemen.

"Servants such as your butler should be here too," he said

as he took the paper from Phillip. The list contained about thirty names.

"Will your Mr. Marsh want to be known as a medium or just as your friend?"

*Your Mr. Marsh.* He smiled at that. "As my friend, I suppose, to start with. Perhaps he could discuss his...work after a while."

"Your smile seems fond, Robert. Are you truly friends with this man?"

Court was going to deny it but shrugged instead. "Yes, I suppose I am. Dreadfully unprofessional, of course."

"If you trust him, then it isn't, indeed. You have a very good instinct for that sort of thing. Lily would tell me stories about how you seemed to know when someone was lying. It was almost a supernatural ability."

Court had heard that sort of thing before but considered that to be the same sort of mystical claptrap as the fraudulent mediums. "She was biased, and the truth is that I observe people, that is all. And I observe that you, my friend, need to eat heartier meals."

He shook Phillip's hand, glad that he'd come, even if the visit did nothing to find Lily's killer. He still missed his cousin and seeing her fiancé again reminded him of her life—Court felt glad to recall more of her than her dreadful death.

# Chapter Ten

The party was arranged for three days hence, which was short notice, but Court didn't have much time away from work. He spent hours comparing the names to the stories he'd got from Lily. She had not met many people in London, thank goodness. He also went to two more séances held by Marsh.

Some of the talk was annoying, and the way Marsh spoke of mystical veils parting was almost enough to make him want to roll his eyes, but he'd lost the fury he'd felt when he'd begun looking into the matter of Marsh.

The participants who'd lost loved husbands, wives, children and friends seemed to grow lighter after one of these sessions with Marsh. And he tended to pull each aside and allow them to talk to him, pour out their grief at their loss and their relief to know their missing love was safe. It wasn't all claptrap and babbling.

Court left the first meeting early but waited on a street corner not far from Marsh's lodgings. Sure enough, Marsh came quickly into view and didn't seem surprised to see Court.

"You are going to have to find another way to make a living, you know. Lord Markham is after you."

Marsh sighed. "I like Lady Markham."

"Her money, more likely."

Marsh froze, hand on key. "*Her*. I like her. She's gracious and pleasant. Yes, she always introduces me to her friends, but the truth is, I like Lady Markham."

They were in his apartment now, and Court noticed a gold guinea on the table. The coin reminded him of what Marsh was. He looked at the coin pointedly as he said, "Interesting to know that you can form a bond with your target."

"She is not my target."

"She is not your friend," Court shot back.

Something seemed to slip in Marsh. He lost the stiff-backed appearance and seemed to hunch into himself. "Are you my friend, Mr. Court?"

The same question Phillip had asked. Court didn't answer this time. He folded his arms and stared into those blue eyes.

Marsh gave a low groan. "You matter to me. What you think matters to me, more's the pity." He sounded disgusted.

Court laughed.

"It's not funny," Marsh said. "It's a bloody pain in the arse."

"Yes it is. What you think matters to me too. We are a pair of idiots."

"It does? Truly?" Marsh's eyes went wide, and his smile blazed. "Robert. Thank you for saying that." He reached for Court's hand and pulled him close.

"Pain in the arse, eh?" Court reached around and lightly slapped Marsh's rump.

"Oh, God," Marsh whispered, and Court suddenly understood that it was a groan of delight. Marsh had taken that slap as a promise.

He knew Marsh—Oliver's—rear. It was smooth and round, but when Oliver clenched tight as he reached his orgasm, that muscular part of his body was a thing of power and... Court swallowed, his whole being aroused, not merely his cock, which had come to a full stand inside his trousers.

He needed to see Oliver's back, from his shoulders to his strong calves and that glorious arse especially.

He gave a yank at Oliver's jacket sleeve. "Take this off."

Oliver eagerly complied and threw the jacket over a chair.

"Waistcoat," Court ordered. He put his hand over his cock, to push it into a more comfortable position, but Oliver stopped unbuttoning his waistcoat.

"That is my job." He dropped to his knees and reached for Court's fly.

Court backed away. "Only after you're naked."

Oliver had his clothes off in less than a minute and then went to work on Court's clothes. Court decided to remain passive, allow the other man to work on his buttons and then the dragging off of his clothes.

The air in the flat was warm today, so standing barefoot and naked was pleasant. For several heartbeats they stood facing each other so that only their cocks could brush together.

Then Oliver went to his knees again, encircled Court's legs with one arm so that Robert almost fell over. But his wavering balance was forgotten when Oliver's mouth nuzzled at his groin, then, hot and insistent, enveloped his cock. Up and down, Oliver bobbed his head, mouth sucking so hard it threatened to pull Court right over the edge. Just the sight of the handsome man on his knees, tending to him, sent Court into paroxysms of pleasure.

He was too close, too excited, so he put his hand on Oliver's head. When Oliver ignored the weight of his hand, Court gathered some of the silken hair and gave a pull.

Oliver looked up, mouth glistening, eyes half open. Court smiled and pointed toward the bedroom.

"I have unfinished business." He raised his hand, showing

his palm meaningfully.

Oliver rose at once and grabbed his hand. In his hurry, Oliver almost tripped over his own boots he'd left sprawled on the floor.

The bedroom was dark, and Court paused long enough to light the wall sconce. He wanted to see every inch of Oliver's body. There was oil in that drawer, and he intended to use it everywhere so he could see Oliver's skin glisten. Yes, that would be what he needed.

"On your belly," he ordered, then paused. This wasn't the sort of thing he'd want to insist upon without conversation first. "If you'd rather not..."

Oliver was already sprawled facedown, spread out for Robert's delectation.

Court touched his own cock and knew he was more than ready to put that oil in the spot he craved and push himself into the hot willing body. But they had done this quickly already, gobbled each other up, literally. Something about the way Oliver had described his past lover, a real lover, Court realized, had made him envious. He was more than ready to do the mindless primitive act, but he wanted something new. Something slower and more languid.

He poured the oil onto his hand and rubbed it warm between his palms before he smeared it over Oliver's buttocks. Yes, they flexed nicely as Oliver pressed into the bed.

"Hold still," he ordered. And climbing onto the bed, kneeling over Oliver on one side, he ran his hands over every inch of Oliver's back, the wings of his shoulder blades, the slight grooves on either side of his spine. The muscles moved under his slipping fingers, and he dug in hard when Oliver twisted or turned.

"Not yet," he said to Oliver's pleading moan. When Oliver

surged against the bed, he slapped the writhing buttocks—just hard enough to give him a warning.

Oliver spread his legs, and Court let his fingers slide down between the round glistening cheeks to touch the balls which were already drawn tight against Oliver's body.

There was only the scent of the oil, the harsh breath of both men and the feel of the gorgeous body under his hands. For five minutes at least, he allowed himself to glide and test that flesh, touching Oliver only with the insides of his thighs and his hands, although as he reached up to stroke his shoulders, his penis slid along the slippery back.

Five minutes was a very long time for a man dizzy with lust. Two men. Oliver writhed and bucked hard under Court's slow deliberate strokes. He whimpered, then growled. "Go ahead and slap me silly if you wish, Robert. Just fuck me. Now."

He pushed up onto his hands and knees, presenting himself like a gift. Court allowed himself another long look before he slid his fingers down, sliding between the delicious globes into the clenching warmth.

That opening was too tight. He had to work in one finger carefully, and Oliver gasped, pushing back. He gritted his teeth and managed to slide in another finger.

He gripped his cock with his other hand and leaned in to the inviting tight heat.

They both groaned as Court's cock pushed in past the tight ring. He moved slowly, dragging his fingers over Oliver's oil-slicked back and sides to keep himself from thrusting hard.

This was true fucking. He was inside Oliver, and the thought almost made him lose control.

He did lose that precious command over himself when Oliver reached behind him to grasp Court's hip and pulled him closer.

"Harder," Oliver ordered.

"I won't last."

"Fuck me harder," Oliver snarled.

For a moment, Court considered pulling out and making him beg more politely. No, God, no. He'd let himself go and show the man what he was asking for.

Court thrust himself deep and pulled nearly out before jamming in faster, then again, harder. Such astonishing pleasure. He leaned on Oliver's back, sliding his body over the slighter form under him even as he thrust.

He was so close, so ready to explode.

The sensation began slowly at the base of his spine but then rocketed through him. As the last of the spasms rocked him, he reached around Oliver's body to grasp his cock and pump urgently.

The cock in his fist grew impossibly hard and swelled. Oliver pushed his face into the pillow as he shuddered to his crisis. Good—the man's bellow would have brought the police if it hadn't been muffled.

Still panting, damp with sweat and sweet-smelling oil, Court smiled, then leaned on Oliver's back, not quite ready to break their connection. He rubbed his face on Oliver's slick skin and allowed himself to think of nothing but the pleasure that had soaked into his body.

*How easy this is.* The thought filled him to overflowing, and he didn't understand it at all, because of course, there was nothing easy about carrying on sexual relations with another man. The situation was fraught with peril and doomed to extinction. He and Oliver could not continue to carry on this way, coming together at every possible opportunity, forgetting all else and losing themselves in each other.

Court reminded himself of all the reasons they could not continue to meet. Hadn't this very episode begun with his annoyance that he'd felt charmed by a fraud of a medium? And then there was the matter of other broken laws. Someone, perhaps a neighbor, would begin to notice their comings and goings, and reputations were as fragile as spun glass. As an officer of the law, he should certainly eschew committing crimes. Court would soon be called on to show some forward momentum on Marsh as a case. What could he provide to Hardy without truly exposing Oliver?

But despite these niggling fears that clustered like gnats at the edge of his consciousness, Court couldn't and didn't want to banish the euphoria that filled him at this precise moment. *How easy this is, to lie with a lover and drowse away an autumn afternoon. I have never been more content.*

# Chapter Eleven

If there was one skill that Oliver had perfected during his time as a medium, it was the ability to understand the general sentiment in a room and manipulate it to his best advantage. As he was introduced to Phillip Hasel's friends, he recalled the bit of background Court had provided on each man.

"Good afternoon, Mr. Barrington." He shook the banker's hand and gazed into his eyes, waiting for the onrush of dread and dizziness that had accompanied each of Lily's last visits. But Oliver saw only sadness in the portly man's eyes and felt a dash of loneliness in his touch, no doubt the result of his broken engagement. Barrington and Hasel were particularly close, both having suffered the loss of a fiancée, though for far different reasons.

"So pleased to meet you, Mr. Parekh." The East Indian physician emitted the faintest scent of incense and a trace of uncertainty. Perhaps this was something he always felt, being a stranger in a cold, wet foreign land.

Oliver waited to feel more, but apparently the ability had vanished again.

"And very pleased to meet you, sir. What is your connection to our Mr. Hasel?"

"Friend of a friend," Oliver replied. "This gathering is an opportunity to widen the range of my acquaintances. You understand what it's like to accustom yourself to a new place and try to build friendships."

"Indeed, I do." Parekh nodded animatedly, his lilting accent rising and falling. "You don't by chance play *Pachisi*, better known to you English as Parcheesi? A few friends and I have started a club. We meet on Saturday afternoons."

"That sounds marvelous. Tell me the details and I'll be certain to stop by some time." Oliver smoothly extricated himself from the eager Mr. Parekh and Phillip Hasel introduced him to another man.

"May I introduce Mr. Edward Dumbarton?"

Oliver felt nothing out of the ordinary as he grasped the shopkeeper's hand, nor did he receive a vision from any of the other three men Hasel introduced him to. But he was able to read from their expressions and the way they carried themselves various inklings about their personalities. Dumbarton's smug, self-righteous manner covered a sense of insecurity. Quentin Arliss was a genuinely happy man, but he seemed curious, as if he wondered why in the world he'd been invited to this party. And so forth.

Oliver took the measure of each man, piecing together what he knew of their backgrounds coupled with their mannerisms and adding in his own bit of sensitivity when he took their hands. This was the first time he'd fully realized—or at least acknowledged—that he'd perhaps always had a touch of his grandmother's gift. He could read people, or rather *feel* them in some elemental way, which had nothing whatsoever to do with sensing the afterlife but perhaps they were related. What a nuisance to have a skill but no notion of how to control it or even understand its basic nature.

There was a moment when Phillip left his side and went to get refreshments. Robert came up beside Oliver. "Nothing?"

He shook his head. "Not so far." He wished he had more to offer than these erratic pulses like a telegraph that worked only in intermittent bursts. Useless.

"Perhaps this acquaintance of Lily's was not someone Phillip introduced her to," Robert suggested. "Maybe a shopkeeper she met while marketing or a hansom driver or servant, someone she was comfortable enough to trust until it was too late."

"Maybe." Oliver had another idea, but he wouldn't bring it up to his friend. The idea that Lily might have had a lover other than her fiancé had occurred to Oliver some time ago, but it was hardly the kind of thing he could discuss with her beloved cousin.

A twitching sensation raced down his spine, and he shifted in irritation. Awful to have an itch in an unreachable spot while in a public place. Oliver took out his handkerchief and patted his sweating brow. This parlor was too stuffy and hot with far too many gentlemen crowding the room. In a moment, he'd make his excuses and step outside to take the air. Escaping the haze of cigar smoke which was giving him a headache would be a welcome relief.

"Mr. Marsh." Hasel's voice interrupted his plans for escape. "I would like you to meet Mr. Thomas Patterson, the curate of St. David's. The church, not the cathedral in Cheapside."

He might have said more, but Oliver was busy trying to stay on his feet. As Oliver turned, the room seemed to spin around him. He was caught in a whirlpool, circling, circling and going down. Sensations and emotions swept over him in a wave and carried him away. Lily again. Her fear, her confusion, her pain and her realization of life bleeding out of her body...and her recognition of her killer. Yes, she knew who he was, so why couldn't she give Oliver a clearer impression of his...

*His face.* Oliver gazed into mild blue eyes behind wire-rimmed spectacles and felt bone-shattering fear.

"Good day, Mr. Marsh. So pleasant to meet you. Isn't it wonderful to share fellowship with friends old and new?" The curate stretched out his hand and grasped Oliver's before he could flinch away. The moment their flesh touched, the feeling of terror magnified.

*This is for the best, my dear.* The voice in his mind overlapped with Thomas Patterson prattling on about God's joy in seeing his people spend time together. The tone was the same, a pleasant tenor that should've been soothing, well-modulated, a voice made for speaking from the pulpit, and yet Patterson's voice made Oliver's skin crawl as if covered in maggots.

Unfortunately, the curate was a man who liked to talk while clasping hands with the person he was greeting. Oliver disengaged his hand from the man's moist grip as soon as he could politely do so. He took a step backward and bumped into Robert, who was close behind him.

"Goodness, I feel a bit faint," Oliver said truthfully. "I must step out for a breath of air. Please pardon me." He turned and walked toward the doors leading out to the garden, nearly fleeing from the scene.

He fumbled with the latch on the door, desperate to get away. Robert pulled his hand away and opened the door for him, ushering Oliver outside.

The flagstone walkway had been swept bare of leaves, but more were drifting lazily down from the trees in the garden. Oliver felt Robert take hold of his elbow and steer him down the path to a bench. He dropped down onto it, the stone cool and a bit moist even through his trousers.

Robert stooped to look into his eyes. "What is it? Was that the man? The curate?" He sounded incredulous, unable to believe a man of God would have anything to do with the murder of his cousin. One would think as a police inspector Robert Court would be unsurprised by the depths of depravity in any man's heart.

Oliver dipped his head. "I'm almost certain of it." He paused. "No. I *am* certain of it, as much as if he'd told me so. That mild-mannered Christian spoke the last words Lily every heard. What I don't know is the why of it or how it came about."

Robert dropped to his haunches, squatting before Oliver sitting on the bench. "Thomas Patterson. I looked into his background only a little. He has been at St. David's as curate for almost a year. Prior to that... Well, I must admit I didn't look back that far."

"If the impressions Lily had were true, then there have been others before, and he means to kill again." Oliver leaned forward, forearms resting on his knees. This put his face only inches from Robert's. Close enough to lean forward and steal a kiss if they were someplace more private—or at least a comforting embrace.

"I need to find where he came from and if any suspicious disappearances or deaths occurred in his proximity." He looked into Oliver's eyes. "What did you hear or sense exactly? Anything different than before, anything that would provide more clues? I can't just shoot the man unprovoked, much as I might like to. So we must find some irrefutable evidence against him."

Oliver nodded. He glanced over Robert's shoulder at the french doors leading into the parlor. He didn't know if he could bear to walk through them and face that onslaught of feeling again. "What will you tell Phillip? I don't think you can tell him the truth. He'll want to rip the man apart with his bare hands—if he even believes me."

Robert's knees cracked as he straightened. "We will tell him nothing about this, say the experiment was fruitless. Do you think you can go back in now? We must stay a little longer. If you beg off on account of illness, Phillip will guess something has happened."

Oliver rose and felt less dizzy than he'd expected, although there was still a throbbing in his temples. "Yes, I can fake bonhomie for a little while longer. I am a consummate fraud, after all, as I think we've already established." He managed a weak grin and was rewarded with Robert's rare smile.

"If you feel faint or ill, do let me know." Robert guided him down the path with a hand on the small of his back. How soothing that small gesture was.

"I will. Well before I am sick on Mr. Hasel's carpet, I promise."

"You stay well clear of the curate, and I'll question the man as thoroughly as I dare without giving him cause for alarm," Robert added before they went inside.

Oliver was quite content to socialize with whichever gentlemen were farthest from Thomas Patterson. But even as he talked with Rajit Parekh and Lionel Barrington, he kept a sharp eye on Court and the curate. He'd half expected Robert to loom over the other man, grilling him unmercifully, and was surprised by the easy manner with which he treated his suspect. It seemed Oliver wasn't the only man here adept at subterfuge. Robert managed an easy charm with Patterson that had the man chattering gregariously.

Oliver's hands were soon full with listening to Barrington drone on about banking while Parekh talked about his obsession with polo. Of the two, the latter topic was slightly more interesting, but Oliver wasn't eager to continue either conversation for long. He was overjoyed when Robert broke off his chat with Patterson and gave Oliver a small nod from across the room.

Oliver found their host and bid him good-bye. "Thank you sincerely, Mr. Hasel, for hosting this afternoon's gathering. It was most entertaining." He leaned in to add in a whisper, "But I'm sorry to say, not enlightening. I have no new information to share."

Robert joined him on the excuse of giving Oliver a ride home, and they said their good-byes to the rest of the company before leaving.

Mr. Hasel accompanied them to the foyer. After a footman had provided them with their hats and coats, he bid the man leave and spoke to them privately. "So nothing of note occurred, Mr. Marsh?"

Oliver considered how ironic it was that now he'd actually had a psychic experience, he was forced to keep quiet about it, lying in reverse, so to speak. "I have nothing to share with you," he spoke semi-truthfully. "I wish that I could give you comfort."

Mr. Hasel's face was tense with emotion. "Lily's last minutes on earth were horrific. If I only knew she now rested at peace, I would feel better. I had just begun to accept her death and now this...this upheaval."

"I'm so sorry." Oliver's response was completely truthful this time.

"I would not have told you at all," Robert added, "but if there's a chance of apprehending the actual killer, I must try before he strikes again."

Phillip nodded. "As I would wish you to, no matter how painful the situation is to me."

When they were out on the street, Oliver looked at Robert. "What now? How do you suggest going about catching this man? Shall we watch him constantly?"

Court frowned. "I don't believe there is imminent danger of him taking action. At least I pray that I am right. Talking to Patterson, I did not get an impression of agitation or distraction such as one might expect from a man about to commit murder. I can hardly imagine he would attend a social event such as this if his plans for killing were imminent. Lily's death took place on Guy Fawkes last year. I have a feeling that night has a special significance to Patterson. For now, I plan to learn all I can about his past and maybe find something to use against him."

"Good. I'll help you. And as for your hunch, I suppose one wouldn't get far as a police inspector without learning to listen to that inner voice."

Robert hailed a cab, and they climbed in.

"To the library?" Oliver suggested. "I find back issues of newspapers an invaluable research aid."

Robert checked his watch. "Too late in the day. Nor can I stop by the police station and look up records without arousing suspicion. Patterson was extremely vague about his previous employment. I hope to learn more from the vicar or whoever hired him as assistant curate. His references might give us a clue about his background. Place of birth, for one thing, and that would be a good place to start." He glanced at Oliver. "You look worn. Do you wish me to drop you off at home?"

"No. I couldn't possibly relax. I want to help with this."

Robert gave the direction to the driver, and soon they'd traveled the few blocks to the churchyard. Oliver was careful to avert his eyes from the site of Lily's death. He didn't need yet another vision of what she'd gone through.

The churchyard gate was locked. Not even the gardener in sight. They would have to return during regular hours the following day.

*The Psychic and the Sleuth*

Oliver and Robert climbed back into the cab, and Robert gave him a sideways glance. "Would you care to stop by my house for a bit? We could continue to discuss the case and try to come up with a firmer plan."

Oliver bobbed his head. He would no more have returned to the solitude of his flat than face a gallows right at this moment. He was that nervous in the aftermath of his encounter with Patterson.

"Yes, please. I would love to visit." He hesitated, then added, "Touching that man's hand was...indescribable. Something akin to plunging my hand into a nest of squirming snakes. I felt Lily's dying fears again, but I also felt... How shall I put it? I believe I felt the very *nature* of the man, and it was both deadly and painfully bleak. Such a miserable, tormented soul."

Robert's jaw tightened. "I feel no sorrow for him. In fact, if I weren't sworn to uphold the law, I should probably take matters into my own hands and end his miserable existence."

"It sounds a satisfying and productive plan," Oliver agreed. "But we are civilized men, are we not?"

"Unfortunately." Robert settled back into the seat, his knee bumping against Oliver's, who faced him. "In my line of work, there are instances in which necessary force may be taken and a dangerous criminal brought to immediate justice. But that usually involves the criminal brandishing a weapon and threatening officers or the public. To eliminate an unarmed curate on a suspicion would not go over well." He sighed. "So we'll bide our time and do what we can to stop him and bring him to justice by more conventional means."

Oliver was content to fall silent then and nearly drifted into a doze as the cab swayed across town. When it drew to a stop, his eyes flew open. He was excited to see Robert Court's home.

He imagined it spartan and extremely neat but containing a secret vice, like silken sheets or something. But no, for a housekeeper might look askance at such a luxury in the home of her squarely middle-class employer, and Robert was not the type to invite curiosity. Plain cotton sheets it would be.

Robert paid the cabbie and led the way up the stoop to his front door. As he fitted the key to the lock, high-pitched excited yapping came from inside.

"You have a dog," Oliver said needlessly.

"Jock. He's a Highland terrier." As Robert opened the door, the little dog hurtled through and leaped up against Oliver's legs. "I'm afraid he's poorly trained. My fault. I've not been around enough, and when I am, I spoil him. You don't mind dogs, do you?"

Oliver had already stooped to accept Jock's joyous welcome. He received a faceful of licking tongue and doggie breath. "I love them. My father didn't, so I could never have one growing up and I always imagined one of the first things I'd do when on my own would be to get a mongrel. But somehow I haven't got around to it."

"This is Jock III." Robert crouched beside him and ruffled the dog's wiry fur. "I'm not very original. I've named him after a series of family pets. The first Jock died of old age. The second ran into the street and met an untimely end there. This Jock is only a little over a year old and very full of energy, as you can see."

Oliver found himself inexplicably reduced to baby prattle, cooing at the slobbering dog. "Who's a good lad? Yes, you are."

Robert rose, smiling. "Do come in."

After they were inside, he closed the door behind them. Oliver looked around the quiet foyer, noting the stately grandfather clock and an indifferent landscape on the wall. He received an impression of once plush, now rather worn, middle-class comfort.

"Was this your family home?"

"Yes. My parents are both gone now, and my siblings moved on to lives of their own. Sometimes I think I should sell and buy a smaller place with fewer memories attached. But..." He shrugged. "It's easier not to make a change, so I find I keep putting it off. I suppose I'm comfortable here."

"There's nothing wrong with that. This is certainly more pleasant than my rooms." Oliver handed Robert his hat and coat. "Have you no servants?"

"My housekeeper doesn't live in. She and a maid do the cleaning, and she prepares me a meal to reheat later. It suits me not to have staff around."

Oliver nodded. "That is why I rent rather than live with my mother. I must have privacy." He gave Robert a sly grin and noted the quick glimmer of a smile curving the other man's lips.

"I'll put Jock into the back garden to do his business, but after we've had a cup of tea, I hope you don't mind if we take him on a walk. He lives for his daily constitutional."

"I would like nothing better than to walk your dog with you." Despite the gloomy pall his encounter with the curate had cast over him, Oliver suddenly felt very sunny. Robert had invited him to his home. That was a significant development. Perhaps he was beginning to see the possibility of them spending more time together even after Lily's killer was apprehended.

Oliver could already see the pair of them playing chess of a winter evening—he'd even learn to appreciate chess if it would entertain Robert. They would walk the dog in the park on Saturday afternoons. As far as anyone seeing them together might be concerned, they would simply be two good friends.

Robert gestured to the room off the front hall. "If you'll wait in the sitting room, I'll brew some tea."

"I'll help you. I'm a dab hand at tea brewing *and* placing biscuits on a plate. We bachelors must learn to do for ourselves, eh?"

Robert chuckled and led the way to the kitchen, a cozy room that rather reminded Oliver of the kitchen in the house he grew up in. "My family home was like this," he said as he opened the tin and proved his agility with biscuit placement. "My mother may have been more devastated at losing her home than she was at my father's passing. I know I was."

"You didn't get along?"

"To put it succinctly, no. But to elaborate, I could never be the kind of son he expected me to be, and I was too foolish and stubborn to play the part adequately. I insisted on flying against the wind."

Robert poured hot water from the kettle on the hob into a flowery teapot. Oliver was fascinated by the contrast of those large, very masculine hands on the delicate porcelain. Robert peered into the pot and put the lid in place. "It's easier for some than others to wear a straitjacket. I suspect you recognized your special inclination at a young age and accepted what you could not deny. Am I right? Meanwhile, I fought against my desires for many years until I was exhausted from the battle."

Oliver's curiosity was piqued. This was the most open Court had been with him. "And your first encounter?"

"Other than a brief fling with a boy in my form—but every British schoolboy probably has a similar tale—I kept strictly celibate except for the pleasure of my own hand, until I was twenty-four." He stared at the steam rising from the teapot spout. "I was terribly drunk one evening and wandering through a certain park. Of course I'd heard the rumors of the kind of activities that went on there after dark. Later, I would tell myself I was attacked, set upon, violated by a stranger, but I'd actually found exactly what I was looking for."

"How long before you finally accepted that aspect of yourself?"

He shrugged. "I struggle to accept it still. I am a man of the law, after all, and am breaking the law every time I..." He glanced at Oliver.

"Do you wish to hear my opinion on morality and man's laws versus God's laws?" Oliver asked. "I believe much of what we're forced to swallow is utter poppycock. People pretend to know what is moral and right based on the Bible, an ancient tome with suspect beginnings and myriad possible interpretations. I believe in the doctors' code, 'first do no harm', and think society should be based on it. If a person's actions aren't harming another, then that other person should keep his or her nose out of the first person's bloody business."

Robert chuckled, a rich sound that sent a ripple of pleasure through Oliver. "I believe you're wiser than I, Oliver Marsh."

Oliver smiled. He snapped off half of a ginger biscuit and held it over Jock's nose. The dog sat on his haunches, pointing like a setter and gazing with intent eyes at the treat. "It is all right to feed him, isn't it?" The biscuit had left his hand and been engulfed by the dog before Oliver heard Robert's answer.

"Not too many, though. Terriers are prone to getting a bit barrel-shaped in their old age. I want to keep Jock the third in fighting trim."

"Well then, we should let our tea wait and go walk this fine lad," Oliver said. "You want to go outside, don't you? Yes you do." It was impossible not to lose all dignity when gushing at a dog.

"Very well," Robert agreed, and they abandoned their tea to

put on their coats and Jock's leash.

The white dog pulled against the leash until he was wheezing, leaning into the restraint and tugging his master's arm to a nearly ninety degree angle. "Jock," Court admonished in a stern voice, but the terrier was heedless, focused on pigeons that were always just ahead on the sidewalk.

"You can see I'm hopeless at controlling him," Robert said. "The first Jock was much better trained, but that was because my brother worked with him."

"He seems happy enough. What does it matter if he's a little disobedient?" Oliver found it quite amusing that a man who liked playing the dominant had so little sway over his own real-life pet. For himself, Oliver would love to obey Robert's commands and earn a sharp reprimand if he didn't.

As they walked, he surveyed the neat terraced houses, as portly and stuffy as a row of bankers. It was a comfortable neighborhood, quiet and well-behaved. Made Oliver want to take a stick and run it over the iron fence railings just to make a little noise. Exactly the sort of behavior he'd been prone to as a boy. Some things were hard to outgrow.

"Do no harm." Robert broke their companionable silence. "That is an excellent code to live by. But I must ask you, do you feel you're doing no harm when you purport to be a medium and take money from people for a service you aren't really providing?"

The warm, friendly mood burst like a bubble. Were they back to discussing this again? Oliver suddenly realized Robert might not be able to ever move past his fraud.

"I've told you I provide what my clients need, so no, I don't feel particularly guilty about, uh, misrepresenting my abilities to them."

"You mean lying to them."

"Yes. That."

"But I think you do." Robert tugged on the leash, drawing Jock back. The dog walked sedately for several paces, then resumed his headlong lunge. "I believe you know it's wrong, or why else would you fear an investigation? Very soon now I'm going to be expected to give my superior something on you. I've led him to believe I'm close to being able to expose you."

Oliver's stomach ached as if he'd received a blow. "What will you tell him?"

"I honestly don't know. I suppose I'll say I couldn't uncover sufficient evidence after all."

"Will the department leave me alone then?"

"You've come to the attention of the wrong people, I'm afraid. Too successful with certain members of the upper crust."

Oliver sighed. Lady Markham and her friends, of course.

Robert stopped walking and turned to look at Oliver. "You can't win this fight. If I can't produce evidence, there are others who would manufacture it, or merely denounce you in the press to warn your clients away." Robert gave a halfhearted tug on the lead, but now that they'd stopped, Jock was taking the opportunity to urinate on a hitching post. "I'm telling you that one way or another your business will be shut down—even if you were truly using clairvoyant gifts. You need to consider another line of work."

Oliver's chest constricted, and heat flamed in his cheeks. He'd already come to the same conclusion but would argue anyway. "I'm good at what I do, and I help people. I don't see any harm in that."

"We disagree, but more to the point, you can't stay in that...profession." Robert traced the wrought-iron scroll in the fence beside him. "We must consider how your skills could be put to another use. Perhaps you could offer similar services but advertise them a different way. Don't claim a psychic ability. I wonder if it would be possible to offer yourself as a counselor, something like a curate but without the religious connotations."

Oliver was flabbergasted. He hardly knew how to respond to Robert attempting to rearrange his life. "It seems you've given this some thought."

"As a matter of fact, I have. I don't wish to see you in trouble."

What could one say to such a gesture of thoughtfulness? "Thank you. I'll take what you say very seriously and give it due consideration."

He was anxious to change the topic and knew bringing up the murder case was a certain way to distract Robert. "I've had a thought concerning a way to perhaps direct Tom Patterson into a net of our devising."

"Yes?" Robert said.

"I shall join the congregation and keep a close eye on the man. You already know I'm nearly convinced that your cousin was not his only victim. If I watch him, I might find something to implicate him. Or at least I'll be able to stop him before he strikes again."

Robert shook his head. "No."

"Have you thought of another plan?"

"Not yet, and this idea of yours will do with modification. I shall keep watch on him, not you."

"I don't see why I can't keep an eye on him. I'm the one who picked him out of that crowd of men." Oliver scowled and began to walk again. Jock, who apparently hated anyone else to lead the walking party, immediately stopped sniffing at a bush and skittered ahead of Oliver.

One second, Oliver was strolling down the street. The next, he was pressed to a brick wall, a solid weight against his back, hard, his arm twisted behind, almost to the point of pain. Jock was at his side, barking.

"Do you see?" Robert's voice was in his ear. "You are strong in your way, but you are not a fighter. I have the training for this sort of thing."

"Ugh," Oliver said. His cheek grazed the cold brick, and he couldn't move. Far too predictably, his cock began to stir. And even more intriguing, he could swear that he felt a similar change in the body pressed to his back.

Nearby, a lady gave an angry cry. "I shall call the police. You take your hands off him."

Robert released Oliver's arm and backed away. "No need to be alarmed, ma'am, just giving a demonstration of defensive methods."

Oliver turned around and gave the lady and her maid a nod and smile. The two women walked on without looking back. Oliver swept the dust from his jacket and trousers in a marked manner. "That was unfair," he muttered.

"Attacks often are." Robert gave a tug on the lead. "Hush, Jock."

"All right, you win. You keep watch over Mr. Patterson." Oliver began to walk once more, and Jock, wheezing against his collar, frantically pulled out front.

"I intend to, and I'll start as soon as possible. I believe I will go to him for religious training."

"He's only a curate."

"A very pious one, I've heard."

Oliver gave a small snort of disgust. "Another example of how a man's public image means nothing." He tilted his head and looked at Robert. "Take you, for example. I imagine most who meet you think you a law-abiding, rather chilly sort of a man."

"I am. Law-abiding, at any rate."

"Mr. Court. We've already discussed the fact that you and I break several laws every time we are alone together." He couldn't help smiling. "And I was just reminded of how hot-blooded you are as you threw me against that brick wall." He stopped and pointed to his face. "Look. I swear that's an abrasion from your attack."

Robert leaned close to examine him. His gloved thumb gently rubbed Oliver's cheek. "Barely reddened."

Oliver, unnerved by the slight touch, began walking again. "Nevertheless, Court, I shall pay you back."

"Shall you?" Robert laughed. "I should like to see you try."

"Keep your eyes open when we return to your home, then. In fact, you might wish to learn to sleep with your eyes open." He cursed himself after he said that. Robert would think he was inviting himself to stay the night.

But Robert only nodded. "I enjoy a challenge."

By unspoken mutual agreement, they returned to Robert's house, walking as quickly as Jock could wish.

In the parlor, Robert unclipped Jock's lead, dragged off his coat and waistcoat, and stood in his shirt sleeves.

He looked toward the kitchen. "Very well, Mr. Marsh, it's time for tea."

"No tea." Oliver's words came out as a gasp. He was caught in a haze of lust. Lord, they hadn't even touched since he'd been pushed face-first into a wall.

"Yes, I imagine it's cold and horribly stewed by now,"

Robert said cheerily. Oliver understood that the bastard was simply teasing him by pretending to be putting off what would happen between them. They must touch very soon, or Oliver would begin to howl as fiercely as Jock.

But what on earth? Robert began dragging a large footstool to the corner of the room. Its armchair followed. He grunted as he hauled the massive chair away from the center of the parlor.

Oliver crossed his arms and watched. Curiosity dissipated some of his aroused tension. "What the devil are you doing?"

"Making room. We'll settle this matter once and for all. I don't want to break the furniture."

Oliver grinned as he pulled off his jacket, folded it and laid it on Robert's, which was also neatly folded. His anticipation began to rise again. "You are larger, it is true. But I have been running from bullies for years. I am faster, I'll wager." Before he could finish unbuttoning his waistcoat, Robert was on him, pulling him down and pinning him to the carpet.

They had to banish Jock, who wanted to join in the wrestling. By the time Robert returned from pushing the dog out the door, Oliver had stripped off all of his clothing. He stood with his arms out, ready to grab at Robert should he come near.

But Robert only stood, watching him with a level gaze that made Oliver's naked flesh burn hotter than the coals in the fireplace.

"One kiss," Robert said huskily. "One delicious kiss, and then..."

Oliver came to him and brushed his lips over the rough stubble of his cheeks and chin. He turned his head so that their mouths might meet at the perfect angle immediately, and it was as if they'd practiced for years. Oliver shuddered as his body pushed up against the hot solid wall of Robert and the thick erection that slid against his. The kiss deepened and turned sweeter.

He pulled back, panting.

"So that kiss is done?" Robert asked.

Oliver nodded.

Robert held up the leather lead. "Then we shall have our next course, Oliver."

He wrapped the cool leather around his throat, fastening a noose that pulled roughly against Oliver's throat. The constriction made him harder than ever as Robert wrapped the other end around his fist and used the leash to guide Oliver's head wherever he wanted it to go.

"Down on all fours now," Robert commanded. "I'll have you as my pet."

Yes. That was exactly what he wanted to be, curbed and controlled by this masterful man. Oliver dropped to his hands and knees.

"Heel," came the next order, and Oliver crawled meekly behind his master, eyes riveted on the man's black shoes pressing into the carpet with each step. Being completely nude, leashed, crawling, while Robert was still fully clothed, was possibly the most arousing thing he'd ever experienced. Was it possible to reach the pinnacle of release without ever being touched, simply from the sheer intensity of such submission?

What would Robert do if he acted the naughty dog like Jock? Oliver stopped following, digging his palms and knees into the carpet and refusing to budge.

A sharp jerk on the lead caused the leather to cut into his windpipe. He growled in resistance, and a hard hand swatted his behind. Delightful pain.

"I've let one pet get the best of me. I won't lose control over you," Robert declared. He grasped Oliver's chin and stared into his eyes, dominating him with the power of his gaze. "Before we're through here, I shall teach you to sit, roll over and beg for a treat."

Oliver smiled, ready to pant for a hot salty treat right then, but where would be the fun in that? A little discipline first would only sweeten the final reward.

Robert let go of his chin and moved his hand to caress Oliver's hair. In return, Oliver rubbed the side of his face against that hand, offering his affection.

"Lie on your side on the floor, dog."

He obeyed, hands and feet drawn up in a puppy-like manner. Robert rubbed his belly, making his cock twitch, but the man avoided touching that part of him.

"Roll over."

Again Oliver obeyed, making a barrel turn on the floor, then looking expectantly up at his master. He was rewarded with a ruffling of his hair.

"And again." Robert made a fool of him, forcing him to roll across the floor.

Oliver squirmed at the delicious humiliation that aroused him so greatly, he felt nearly blinded by lust and devotion. He'd taken on roles with lovers in the past, but nothing to compare with this play.

"Face down now and lift your arse into the air."

He literally held his breath in anticipation as strong hands stroked his back, then settled on his buttocks, squeezing them, pulling them apart, delving between. Would it happen now? Would his master move behind him and drive into him? His hole clenched and released in spasmodic bursts. He ached to be filled and whimpered his need into the carpet.

"Oh, you're a hungry little dog, aren't you? What perverse

desires swirl around inside you? Come then, up on your haunches. Sit."

Oliver scrambled upright, settling back on his heels and looking up into Court's gleaming eyes, then down to his crotch. The man's arousal was at his eye level, pressing like an iron bar against his trousers. Oliver lolled out his tongue and panted a little to demonstrate his eagerness.

"Will you beg now? Hold up you paws and ask for what you desire."

Curved hands before his chest and a pathetic whine in his throat, Oliver played the desperate dog to perfection—the begging pose, the sad eyes promising complete devotion forever.

Robert opened his fly with deliberation and pulled out the thick meaty flesh, cupping his cock in the palm of his hand. Oliver started to shuffled forward on his knees, reaching for it.

"Not yet. Beg just a little more. I love the sound."

Oliver obliged. He licked his lips, then whined softly, gazing into Robert's face with pleading eyes.

"Christ, what a beautiful creature you are. Come then and have a taste."

Oliver leaned forward and swirled his tongue over the engorged tip. He hummed in appreciation, then opened his mouth and engulfed his master's cock in heat and wetness. He swallowed it deep, couldn't help it, because Robert suddenly thrust forward, filling him to the point of choking.

Robert grasped his head and began to fuck his mouth with such strength and fury that all Oliver could do was hold on and try not to drown. He grasped the other man's hips, warm, firm flesh beneath his hands, and completely filled his mouth, his throat. The musky scent and taste of his master filled his senses. The sudden assault should've felt demeaning and pitiless, but Oliver loved it. He couldn't help himself. He craved this sudden storm of violence, and Robert knew that about him, knew him all too well. The man clutched his head, grunting and thrusting, then exploding in a warm shower that slid down Oliver's throat.

Eyes watering, he swallowed, lost in a fog of lust so strong it shook him to the core. His own cock was swelling and straining, ready to release at the slightest touch.

Robert shuddered and groaned. He gave one push before withdrawing his cock, leaving Oliver empty and wanting more. Oliver gazed at his master's ecstatic expression, the slack mouth and eyes fluttering open to look down at him. The faux dog gave another soft, begging whimper.

Robert smiled and smoothed back his hair. "Very good. You deserve a treat."

He dropped to his knees before Oliver and reached for his cock, but he didn't let go of the leash that coiled around Oliver's neck. As he rubbed Oliver's cock with long, slow strokes, he tightened the leather so it constricted his windpipe. Oliver groaned as dark spots danced across his vision and his head grew light. He felt his consciousness receding and his moment of epiphany growing. The gathering tension in his balls roared through him in a powerful surge just as he began to black out. The power of his climax left him shaking and weeping on the floor, his spending splashed across his belly.

Robert cooed over him then, wiping his stomach with a pocket handkerchief and loosening the noose around Oliver's neck. He stroked his hair and kissed his mouth. "Was I too rough? I'm sorry. You just make me so... I could hardly help myself."

"No. It was...fine." Such a silly, weak word, but amazing, stupendous, fantastic, astonishing weren't nearly enough to describe his feelings either. Oliver smiled. "It was exactly what I wanted, what I needed. Thank you."

"Good. I would not ever want to truly hurt you or make you feel less than human. It is merely a game, after all."

"Yes," Oliver agreed, but he knew better. There was a delicate balance of power between them. In life they might behave as equals, discussing the details of the case and coming to agreement about what should be done, but in lovemaking Robert would always be the man in control. That was exactly where Oliver wanted him to be.

Oliver reached out and touched the other man's cheek, felt the scrape of stubble against his palm. "That was a wonderful game, but now let us resume kissing for a while, shall we?" He snuggled against the other man, kissing his lips, his jaw, his throat, while unburdening him of his clothing piece by piece.

After they were both naked at last, they had a long leisurely wrestling match on the living room floor before they were both finally sated. They lay entangled with one another in a sprawl of limbs and sweaty flesh. As Oliver drifted into sleep, he thought that he would gladly curl up on this man's hearthrug and be his pet for the rest of his life. The control he allowed Robert, the blessed feeling that someone strong had him in hand, meant he might let all of himself fly free. He slept and dreamed of the exhilarating, ridiculous fun they shared.

# Chapter Twelve

Robert dozed, then woke up next to Oliver. He wondered how many bruises they'd have to show the next day. Jock's lead was still wrapped around the sofa's claw foot, and the sight of it made him grimace with lust as he remembered applying it like a whip to Oliver's bare backside at some point during their escapades.

He lay on his belly on the rough carpet. Oliver's face was turned away, but those slim hips wiggled. "I know you're awake and watching me."

Robert hiked himself up on an elbow. "Truly?"

Oliver twisted around, and grinning, he glanced down at Robert's cock. "No. I usually can't read your thoughts. Although on occasion..." His words were lost in a big yawn as he sat and stretched his arms over his head. "It's quite late. I should return to my rooms."

The way Oliver watched him from the corner of his eye, Robert wondered if he hoped to cadge an invitation to stay the rest of the night.

Robert rose and slid on his trousers without his undergarments. He'd already passed a full night asleep with Oliver Marsh. Waking in the morning with the man in his arms had been a pleasant experience. Too pleasant. He'd best not grow used to such things.

He reached for his shirt. The clock on the mantel chimed, reminding him of the late hour. Oliver should go soon, or the night would slip past them both.

On the other hand, he argued with himself, it would be almost impossible for Oliver to find any transportation this time of night.

He cleared his throat. "You may stay here if you wish."

Oliver was through the parlor door almost at once. Robert found he smiled at the other man's eagerness.

Followed by a yawning Jock, Robert walked down the hall and up the stairs, where he found Oliver peering into the bedrooms. Oliver entered into the room that had been the nursery for Robert and his long-dead brother. He sat on the narrow little bed.

Robert watched from the doorway. He'd thought himself ready to push the man out the door but now was strangely disappointed to see that Oliver didn't expect to share a bed with him.

"Good night, then." He nodded and walked toward his own room. Footsteps pattered after him, and Oliver was right behind him.

"I had to make it appear as if I slept there. For your housekeeper," Oliver explained. He was already shedding the clothes he'd put on.

Of course. He was well versed in the art of trickery. Robert was also good at keeping his secrets—but deception seemed to come as naturally as breathing to Oliver.

He banished these depressing thoughts as he stripped, then climbed onto the tall bed. The moment Oliver slipped in next to him, Robert realized he was wide awake again. He moved close to kiss Oliver. They kissed and kissed and carefully touched each other. They didn't fuck but brought each other off with slow strokes of the hand.

Robert wrapped himself around Oliver's body and fell asleep with a smile on his face.

He woke in an empty bed. Even Jock had abandoned him. Oliver's cheery voice blended with Mrs. Lally's high soprano. Their laughter floated up the stairs.

Robert considered getting up but wasn't sure he wanted to have to explain his unexpected houseguest to his housekeeper.

A few minutes later, Oliver appeared in the doorway, fully dressed and carrying a tray that contained toast and tea. "I told Mrs. Lally you had a morning head from too much brandy."

Robert pushed himself up and leaned against the pillows. "She knows I don't drink to excess."

"She wasn't hard to convince, Mr. Court. In fact, she seemed glad to know you are human, as she put it." He put the tray on a table by the bed.

"Stop gossiping with my servants."

"You don't want me to find out about your terrible habits."

"Exactly." Robert picked up the tea and closed his eyes at the pleasure of that first sip.

"If you don't mind allowing me to use your facilities, I shall take a bath and be ready to go with you to the library. We should find what we can about Mr. Patterson."

"You shall go to the library, and I will comb through police files."

Oliver dragged a chair from the corner to the bedside and settled the chair next to the bed as if Robert was a patient and he a devoted nurse. "How will you search?"

"I accept that you are right, and I'd guess that his other victims are also women who have been interfered with."

"You will look for young women who've been raped and murdered?" When he wasn't at work as a medium, Oliver did not mince words. Robert decided he liked that about the man.

Oliver reached for a piece of toast and a napkin. "Maybe he's not from London. Do you know where else he has lived?"

"That should be easy enough to discover. I don't even have to discuss it with the church elders. I'll simply interview his vicar."

Robert handed him the saucer from his teacup. Oliver rolled his eyes and put the toast on it. "Will you tell the vicar you're an inspector?"

"No. I'll be joining the congregation and spending enough time with both men; I don't want either nervous around me. And the vicar's behavior toward Mr. Patterson might change should he learn what I'm doing. No need to arouse suspicions."

"Shall we meet later?" Oliver's diffident manner didn't fool Robert. The man's interest in his answer was palpable. A trap waited somewhere.

His first response was to refuse. But then again, if he didn't meet Oliver, how would he learn about any information he might uncover at the library?

Robert suppressed a groan. He recognized this pattern of thinking. A wave of stupid panic—quickly followed by nearly as stupid justifications. Oliver would have found his way home despite the late hour. Robert didn't actually need Oliver's help in finding the basic information about Patterson.

Robert drank down the rest of the tea in his cup, though it was too hot. "All right," he said. "Five o'clock at the public house where we supped. The one near your house."

They'd gone there before their second time together, he thought. And now they'd had a third. He contemplated a fourth and fifth.

No, this was not how he'd imagined his life. He hadn't told Marsh—hell, he barely admitted it to himself—but he'd half imagined that perhaps someday he'd meet a woman whom he'd find appealing. It had never happened before, but perhaps such a female existed. They'd have a life and children together, and at the very least, he'd have a home with companionship. He'd supposed he could find a woman who'd not expect much physical affection from him.

But that was a dream he'd had before he'd discovered how much of that sort of affection he wanted to give. The sheer force of what he and Oliver did together. God almighty, it was lightning-hot, too much to even contemplate without a hint of fear—

"You are wearing your sour face, Robert. Would you rather not meet later? I could send you a note with any information I uncover."

"No!" Something close to fear hit him now, and then bemusement. How did the man read him so easily? Robert wasn't like Oliver. He didn't show every emotion on his face. He lowered his voice. "I would like to meet you later. Even if you find nothing useful in the library."

He forced his thoughts back to Lily. He'd asked for time off, but perhaps he could coax the superintendent into allowing him to use Wilford for some surveillance work. The sergeant wasn't gabby and wouldn't mention details of the job to Hardy or Childs, so they would never know it was for the case he'd been warned off of. If Robert asked him to, Wilford would stay quiet until after they gathered the necessary evidence to convict Patterson.

"Finding a way to trap Patterson is my priority, and I shall send word to your rooms if I'll be late."

Oliver nodded. "Yes, keeping watch over Patterson is most

important. I shan't feel slighted if you choose his company over mine."

"Ugh." Robert picked up the last slice of buttered toast and took a bite.

Oliver pushed back his chair and walked to the door. He stopped to smile at Robert, and those expressive blue eyes brimmed with warm amusement. "I'll return to my own lodgings to bathe, then. Don't forget to act headachy with Mrs. Lally. It shouldn't be difficult, given your present mood."

He was gone without a backward glance. Robert felt slightly ruffled, as if he'd been denied the chance to control the situation—or as if he'd hoped for a fast kiss of farewell from Oliver.

"Do not allow me to turn into a sentimental fool," he told Jock and dropped the crust to the floor for the dog. He stood and winced at a pain in his thigh. Last night had taken its toll—Oliver gave as good as he got.


Court was out the door and on his way nearly as quickly as Oliver. It went against his every instinct not to stick close to the curate and watch his every move. He feared for more victims. But he couldn't be in several places at once, and he had to do the legwork to gather any evidence that would give him an excuse to arrest the man.

He headed for the station, tensing as he reached the imposing stone edifice. He didn't want to go inside, where he'd have to field questions of why he was there and dodge the superintendent. But then, as if God was on the side of the righteous and lending a hand, he spotted Wilford coming down the street. He hurried to intercept him.

"Wilford, may I have a word?" he asked as he caught up

with the hulking man. Even not dressed in rough dockworker clothing for his undercover assignment, Wilford would still appear intimidating to one who didn't know him.

"Yessir. We'll walk up the street a bit." Wilford accepted Court's request literally without breaking stride. "What's the matter, sir? I could tell the other day you were preoccupied, and now you're taking this time off."

"Will you help me with a case I'm exploring on my own time? And can I trust you to keep the details from Hardy?"

One thick brow shot up. "Sir, you have to ask?"

Court nodded. "Good man." He quickly filled in Wilford on all the details of the case he could without mentioning Oliver's psychic input. Instead, he put it forth as following a hunch. He knew Wilford understood the value of an investigator's gut feeling.

"I plan to go to this Thomas Patterson's birthplace—I believe I know where it is—and learn all I can about the man, but I'm afraid to leave him unwatched. I wondered if you could do two things for me. Check through case files for anything concerning missing, raped or murdered women. Any unexplained deaths, for that matter, such as suspect suicides. Look for any pattern you might find. I realize it's a tall order and one that might raise suspicion from Hardy if you were caught." He hesitated. "Look for deaths that occurred on or close to Guy Fawkes Day."

"Leave the little blighter to me. I'll invent a reason to be looking. What else?"

"I highly doubt our suspect would carry on his nefarious doings by light of day, but when you have an opportunity, might you go and keep an eye on him? And keep notes of any women he speaks to."

Wilford tipped his shaggy head. "Consider it done, sir. I

always had my doubts about the halfwit that swung for your cousin's death, but it weren't my place to say the investigation was shoddy. If you feel you're on to something, sir, I'm the man to help out. Hardy be damned."

Robert was taken aback by that. The two of them had never spoken openly about the superintendent before. "Thank you. I'll return the favor whenever you need me."

Robert bid his friend good-bye and headed for the train station. His chat with Patterson at Hasel's party had yielded a few hard facts like rocks in the midst of a swirling stream of vagueness. Naturally the curate hadn't been willing to divulge much about where he'd come from when Robert questioned him about his history. "A small village not too far from London" could be any one of hundreds of places, and who knew if even that much was true. But Patterson had accidentally mentioned a few pertinent details that Court was quite certain he hadn't intentionally dropped.

He'd talked about the stench of paper mills and how they polluted the rivers on which they were located, then spoke at length about the living conditions of millworkers and the dangerous conditions their children labored under. Court felt fairly certain he'd come from a mill town, which limited his search a little. But the curate had also let slip his fondness for walking in the hills and touring ancient Roman ruins—another element that narrowed his search still further.

It wasn't until this morning that Court had remembered the last bit of information that saved him the nuisance of tracking down paperwork concerning Patterson's history and perhaps having to bribe someone to take a look at it. Information which might be false at any rate.

Instead, he recalled the odd look on Patterson's face as he spoke cryptically about an angel standing sentinel. "It was as if

*The Psychic and the Sleuth*

the village lay in the shelter of its great wings and I'd pray for protection or deliverance for those little children, but alas, the mills still continue to grind on."

An angel? At first Robert had thought Patterson meant it figuratively, but he'd awakened this morning with the idea that the angel was a statue. Then he suddenly remembered hearing about a natural landmark, a remarkable, huge angel-shaped outcropping on the hillside above the town of Grayfeld-on-Severn.

Robert boarded the train heading there, and within the hour, he disembarked at the station just outside the village. The stench floating from the mills on the river was enough to force him to cover his nose with a handkerchief until he grew used to it.

A short walk took him to the town square, which was bordered by a meeting hall, a public house and a church. Robert headed across the green toward the steepled building. Even from here, he could see the landmark Patterson had inadvertently mentioned, the great rock looming over the village in the bend of the river.

The sign in front of the church labeled it as Holy Redeemer Church of Christ. Once again, God or Fate or pure good luck was with Court. He didn't need to even knock on the door. A man wearing a surplice was tending the gravestones at the side of the building.

Court went around to the side and wove through the uneven rows of drunken headstones until he reached the figure bent over and pulling a creeping vine off one. The man didn't seem to hear him approach or register Court's throat clearing. Finally he called out, "Pardon me, er, Reverend."

The minister jumped, then straightened, putting a hand to his heart. "Good gracious, you frightened me. How can I help you, sir?" He studied Court as a man would any stranger in a town that likely saw few.

Court decided he needn't be too discreet. "How do you do? I'm here to make some inquiries about a man I believe was a resident here."

The old man's eyes grew round. "Indeed? Are you from this area?"

Court shook his head. "I'm from London." He flashed his badge, a sure way to impress a village minister. "I wonder, are you familiar with a man named Thomas Patterson? I believe he grew up here."

The old man shook his head. "Patterson? No. That name is not a familiar one."

"He may have gone by a different name then. It's crucial I learn all I can about him, as I believe he may be a danger to public safety."

"Good gracious," the man repeated. "Would you care to come inside to discuss this? I could offer you a cup of tea."

Robert didn't really want to take the time, but rituals served to open doors in people's memories. "Thank you. I would appreciate a cup. May I ask your name, sir?"

"I am Pastor Ennis Wickwilly. You may refer to me as Pastor."

Robert suppressed the smile that threatened at the outlandish moniker—Wickwilly. "You've lived in this village all your life?" he asked as he followed the man around the back of the church to the rectory.

"I've seen generations come and go and likely it will be my turn to join them soon." The man glanced over at him. "One would think a man of God would welcome his inevitable reunion with the savior joyously, but one finds his heels dig in as he nears the end of his life. Never mind that. You're looking for a man? Who is he again?"

Court liked this frank man and instinctively trusted him. "The truth is, Pastor, that this Tom Patterson may have killed a woman. Perhaps more than one. I wasn't able to find out anything about his life prior to his taking position as a curate at a church in London. I'm not even certain I've chosen the correct village from the clues he let drop in casual conversation, or if there's anything to learn about his behavior in the past. But I had to start somewhere."

The man stopped walking and turned to stare at Court. His unkempt halo of white hair floated around his head in the light breeze. "A murdered woman? Oh my. I can't imagine anyone from our village doing such a thing. And you say this man is a curate?"

His face went still, eyes widening slightly, and Court felt the satisfying snap of a mousetrap closing. He *knew* he was about to hear the piece of information he'd come here for.

"Could you describe what this man looks like?" Wickwilly asked.

"Unfortunately, he's fairly nondescript. Average height and build, blond hair, even features, a mole on his left cheek. He is nearer forty than thirty. I suppose he could be considered handsome but not in a showy way. His manner is slightly awkward, very religious. He wears glasses, and when he speaks, he peers over them and rubs his hands together." He paused to think. "Yet he does have an assurance that might make him the man to turn to if one was feeling unsure about one's faith. Perhaps he's the sort a widow or a woman in emotional crisis would be drawn to confide in."

And here was the part that bothered Court. Why had Lily gone to talk to Patterson that night? Had there been something about her imminent nuptials with Phillip that had caused her concern? What had brought Lily to the curate's dwelling for a chat in the early evening?

The pastor's ruddy cheeks leeched of their color. He walked through the back door into a worn but spotlessly clean kitchen. He indicated a chair for Court, then began to slowly assemble the ingredients for tea. At last, he spoke. "Thomas Cuypers. If it is the man I believe, he didn't change his Christian name, although it sounds as if he has changed churches. After an incident here, he was driven out of our fellowship and fled the community. He was never formally arrested, but everyone believed Rachel Balough's claims."

"What did she say he tried to do to her?"

The man exhaled and pushed a hand through his remaining hair, ruffling it further. "Could we sit and have our tea first? I'm winded and overwhelmed by your news. I need to steady my nerves before I can begin."

Court was impatient. He wanted the story and he wanted it now, but an old man couldn't be rushed through telling a tale. He'd questioned enough witnesses in his time to know that. He walked slowly to match the man's shuffle, waited patiently while he opened the door and led the way into his sitting room that smelt of ancient coal fires and old man. Then he waited some more while Pastor Wickwilly steeped a pot of tea and poured two cups. The pastor's hands shook slightly, and Court wondered if it was emotion or age.

He handed a cup to Court and said, "I haven't thought of Thomas Cuypers in years. In fact, I've tried to forget all about the incident. It's haunted me, for I felt I should've done more for Rachel. It was wrong that she suffered that indignity and Cuypers never answered for the crime."

And now Court's patience was at an end. These teasing

tidbits were starting to annoy him. "What exactly happened, Pastor?"

"Thomas Cuypers was a longtime member of this congregation. He was interested in attending seminary but could not afford to go, so I was giving him instruction, preparing him as best I could for the ministerial profession. I was working so closely with him. How could I not have seen his character?"

"Because he's an excellent deceiver, a chameleon of sorts," Court said. "In my profession, I've met many such men. Their neighbors never have an inkling about their true nature. Did he hurt this girl?"

"He...interfered with her and might have done much worse than manhandle and touch her inappropriately if he hadn't been interrupted. It was Guy Fawkes Night, nearly eleven years ago."

Court felt a fillip of excitement. He'd been right. He must have shown his eagerness, because the reverend paused.

"Please, do continue," Court said.

"You know the sometimes wild nature of that night, the bonfires and rather pagan celebration. We were having a gathering here at the church, an alternative to the more heathen mischief the villagers get up to.

"According to what Rachel told me later, Thomas Cuypers had been meeting with her for some time. They'd had numerous private talks, and she'd begun to view him as a spiritual advisor of sorts." Wickwilly shook his head. "If I'd been more attuned to the needs of all of my flock, I would have known she was in need of counsel."

"One man can't be everywhere at once nor all things to all people. You know that, sir."

The old man sipped his tea, then set the cup aside. "Yes, I

suppose. But to think he was filling her mind with poison in the guise of spiritual direction. It sickens me. At any rate, that night he seduced her into going with him on a walk away from the gathering at the church and up the hillside. To pray at the feet of the stone angel for her guidance was what he told her, but when he got her alone, he began to grope her and...well, you know why a man takes a young woman into the dark alone."

"But he was interrupted before he raped her?" Court was sorry the moment the word left his mouth. The elderly man looked shocked at his use of the rough term.

"Yes. Thank heavens for the revelers who chose to dance around bonfires rather than come to the church. Dickie Peters and some of the other young hooligans were also on the hillside. They heard Rachel's screams and went to her aid. They also beat Cuypers before he slipped away from them.

"Rachel confided all this to me after someone brought her to the church. I sent for the village constable but Cuypers disappeared before he could be arrested. When I think what he might have done to poor Rachel... I'd always assumed he meant to, er, violate her, but I never even considered that he might have killed her afterward to hide his depravity."

"I don't have all the facts yet, but..." Robert trailed off as something occurred to him like fireworks exploding in his mind. The dizzy feeling that Oliver claimed Lily had felt on her deathbed—*before* the curate had bashed the back of her head against the cobblestones. What would cause such disorientation? How would a man who wanted to keep a woman quiet go about it? With a sedative, perhaps placed in her tea. There was the dizziness Marsh had mentioned.

"What else can you tell me about Thomas Cuypers's background, Pastor? Anything you could tell me about his family or his life might help me piece something together."

"His father was a foreman at the mill and died in an accident there. His mother raised the boy as best she could, but I suppose she didn't give the firm guidance he needed. That's the only reason I can imagine for the person he turned out to be. The woman died several years before the incident of which I told you, and Thomas lived in the family house alone after that."

Court considered the facts. Finding out any more about what had shaped Cuypers was not going to go far in helping hunt the man now. He already knew Thomas Patterson was guilty. What he needed was some solid evidence on which he could arrest him—he considered going to that house and planting the evidence himself.

He bid good-bye to the pastor and walked back to the station. Planting evidence? He wondered how far he'd fallen into the gray. The world as black and white, good and bad, was a more comfortable place. But such an existence wouldn't allow a man like Oliver to walk free. And keeping him safe was important, almost as important as capturing Lily's murderer.

# Chapter Thirteen

Oliver felt a little guilty about lying to Robert but not enough to stop himself. He was actually very touched that the man cared enough about him to throw him against the wall and give him a lesson in the danger they were up against. Except Oliver didn't believe Thomas Patterson was a danger to him. The man preyed on defenseless women and apparently sedated them in some way so they wouldn't fight back. He would hardly unleash violence on Oliver unless he felt cornered, and Oliver had no intention of attacking Patterson, even verbally, during his visit. He would simply draw the man out and learn what he could about him.

Oliver only hoped he could be near the curate without suffering another wave of illness such as the man's presence had spawned in him yesterday.

"Lily Bailey, if you want me to help solve your murder, you have to give me a little help." He addressed the dead woman as he neared the church. His muttering earned him a glance from a man passing by, and Oliver smiled and tipped his hat at the man.

He stopped outside the churchyard fence and noted the gate was unlocked today. He let himself inside and wandered around the building until he came to what must be the parsonage behind it. If the vicar lived there, where would the curate room be? Did they share a house? Oliver knew little about the workings of religious life. He'd steered clear of churches ever since he was old enough to resist going with his mother on Sunday.

He walked to the vicarage next to the church. A maid with a dark uniform and dirty apron opened the door. "May I help you, sir?" She had the accents of East London and eyed him sharply. Too alert by half, although she did squint at him. She needed glasses. "I'm here to talk with Mr. Patterson if he's available. Do you know where I might find him?"

"He doesn't live here. That's his residence just behind, next to the stables. But he's in the church today, organizing items for the bazaar." She nodded toward the building. "Go to the left of the sanctuary to the fellowship hall, and you'll find him."

"I see. Is it all right if I go inside and find him?"

"T'isn't my business. His housekeeper might keep track of him, but I don't." Oliver's pulse was racing like Jock pulling against his leash as he mounted the steps to the church and rested his hand on the door latch. He'd managed to walk past Lily's death spot with no ill effects today but didn't know if his luck would hold out when facing Patterson. From his grandmother's writings, it seemed she'd learned to control the effects of her "gift" over the years or at least hide it so well that others didn't know she was suffering from a vision. Now that Oliver knew what the onset of a psychic event felt like, maybe he too could learn to manage it better.

He entered the building, breathing in the scent of candle wax and furniture polish. Beyond another open set of doors was the sanctuary with its rows of wooden pews, altar and cross and the hushed air of mystery that seemed to shroud all religious places. God's house. Oliver nodded in the direction of the altar, acknowledging the deity and asking for a little help dealing with the insane killer he was about to face; then he walked down the corridor toward the great room where the churchgoers gathered to socialize each Sunday.

The room was filled with tables piled with cast-off items for the sale. At the far end, Tom Patterson was bent over a barrel full of old clothing.

No rush of horror or despair flooded through Oliver at the sight of the man, though he did feel a prickle of fear down his spine simply from knowing what Patterson had done. He exhaled and drew another breath, then called out to him. "Mr. Patterson."

The curate straightened and turned toward him, an expression of cheerful goodwill lighting his face. "Yes? Oh, Mr. Marsh. How pleasant and unexpected to see you again. I had no chance to talk to you at Mr. Hasel's gathering." He dropped the shirt he was holding and walked toward Oliver, who resisted the urge to back away. "It is so nice to meet new friends, isn't it?"

"My business depends on it," Oliver said truthfully. "I'd hoped to speak with you on a private matter in your capacity as a curate. Do you have a moment?"

"Yes. I'm expecting someone shortly, but I can chat with you. Let's go into the sitting room."

Oliver breathed a sigh of relief when Patterson didn't try to shake his hand. Just the man's approach sent waves of dread washing over him. There was definitely still something swirling around Patterson—those coiling snakes that Oliver didn't want to touch. "It's a question of faith, which I thought with your biblical knowledge you could give me some guidance on. You must have many people ask for counseling on spiritual matters. I imagine that is a large part of your job."

"If it's a very serious matter, of course the person will want to talk to the vicar, but I have my share of congregants pouring out their troubles to me." He glanced over and smiled, and nausea swept through Oliver.

Patterson led him into a small sitting area and directed Oliver to a seat.

He sat on the stiff-backed chair, swallowed, and began his gambit. "It feels good to be able to help people in trouble. I myself am in a line of work that requires giving aid and comfort. Do you find offering support to grieving widows and the like emotionally draining? Recently I've begun to feel too much, to suffer along with them."

"What exactly is your line of work, Mr. Marsh? Mr. Hasel never mentioned it."

"Because he knew it to be a sensitive subject. As a clergyman, you, for example, might be offended by my chosen profession. I am a medium in the Spiritualist movement. I contact the dead and act as a conduit between them and their living loved ones."

"I see." Patterson's expression went blank, but not before Oliver saw, or imagined he saw, a flicker of disgust. The man's tone was markedly cooler when he resumed speaking. "And what is it you want with me, Mr. Marsh?"

"I must admit to a certain unease about my profession." That was certainly true these days. "What is the church's stance on Spiritualism? I've lately begun to worry about the state of my immortal soul." Give any clergyman a slightly open door and Oliver knew he'd talk for hours on the subject. He prepared for the onslaught with the intention of steering Patterson into channels that might be useful.

"I won't say it's the devil's work, but..." The curate was off, enumerating all the ways Oliver was putting his soul in jeopardy.

After several minutes, Oliver interrupted. "But I feel I'm giving my clients comfort. I'm not saying heaven doesn't exist. Quite the opposite, I'm reassuring them that their loved ones are quite safe and contented on the other side and that they still love them. Don't you find yourself offering similar words of encouragement to people?"

"The ladies...the people I counsel want a Bible-based truth, not some mumbo jumbo invented to appease them." Patterson's tone was so smug it made Oliver want to give him a poke just to see him jump.

"But you also give them comfort and succor when they are distressed," Oliver said. "I've seen in my own work that mourning women or young ladies suffer from hysteria, as the fair sex is prone to do. I imagine you're very good at that."

Seeming blithely unaware of where Oliver was steering him, Patterson continued, "Women do seem to be more likely to want to talk about their problems. Very few men ask for advice. I suppose that is the nature of our arrogant sex."

Oliver forced a smile and layered on another compliment. "I should imagine the younger ladies in particular are eager to address you rather than the elderly vicar. A handsome man such as you must have all the young female parishioners setting their caps for him."

"I have my share, but I discourage such attention. I'm here as their confessor, not a love interest." Patterson's pride in being an object of female attention was obvious, and he seemed not to have noticed that Oliver had focused the conversation on him.

"In my line of work, it's widows," Oliver confided, man to man. "I must divert their interest when they become too...affectionate. Do you ever have a similar problem, and if so, how do you manage it?" He'd laid his snare; now he must carefully draw the noose tighter.

Thomas Patterson leaned forward slightly. He sat across from Oliver, and their knees were nearly touching. The room was quiet, and the feeling of two similar gentlemen sharing confidences wove them together.

"I will admit that sometimes I must quell an eager young woman's advances. They can be quite doggedly determined to achieve their goal of landing a husband. But it is the ones who are more subtle in casting their spells that can be even more difficult to resist."

Was he talking about Lily now? A woman who hadn't been interested in him and had therefore been much more desirable as a conquest? Was that how Thomas Patterson worked?

"Ah yes," Oliver said, "I believe I understand you. Sometimes a very beautiful, pure soul is so desirable. So difficult to resist. Like the sweets one's mother would put on a top shelf and allow only on special occasions."

"A pure soul," Patterson murmured almost to himself. "That's it exactly."

"They are rare and so beautiful," Oliver continued. "A man could hardly be blamed for wanting to pluck such an exquisite blossom."

Patterson looked startled. "Pardon?"

"I meant only that resisting temptation can be very difficult, and that is the other reason I've come to you for counseling. I'd hoped to find someone who could understand my struggle."

The curate's eyes narrowed, and he sat back, the spell broken. "I'm sure I do not know what you're talking about, my good man. I assure you I've not struggled with any 'temptation' such as you suggest."

"No, of course not. I was merely inferring from my own experience. Wrong of me. So sorry if I've offended you in any way."

Patterson seemed to relax. "No offense taken. It's easy for a sinner to imagine his sin in others. We like to believe we share a commonality with our fellow beings."

Oliver knew when it was time to make an exit. He'd coaxed as much from Patterson as he dared for one visit. "I must go now. You've given me enough of your valuable time, and as you said, you have another appointment."

Oliver rose, and so did Patterson.

*Please don't shake my hand,* Oliver thought, but the curate was already reaching out, and there was nothing for Oliver to do except grasp his hand. It was like gripping a skeleton, not because Patterson's hands were bony, but because he felt already dead. A desolate breeze blowing through an abandoned house.

Oliver quickly let go. He caught his breath and steadied himself. "Perhaps we might meet again sometime, Mr. Patterson. I've truly enjoyed our talk and feel edified from listening to you."

He would've liked to have bolted from the room but made his leisurely way out alongside the curate. His patience was rewarded when Patterson offered one more nugget of information before they parted.

"Do come for another talk anytime, Mr. Marsh. I believe you are on a dangerous course with this Spiritualist nonsense, and I would like to help you change that course. It is good to have someone with whom we can talk about intimate things. The world is a lonely place, and secrets we bear alone can become a heavy burden."

Oliver nodded and took his leave, not letting go of his breath until he was safely outside on the church steps with the door closed behind him. Patterson's parting words weren't a confession by any means but were an indication that he wanted to unburden himself. That was something maybe Oliver could work with.

He hurried down the steps and across the churchyard.

"Surely it is Mr. Marsh?" A slightly familiar voice stopped him. A young lady paused just at the gate. A maid stood next to her.

"Ah! Miss, erm."

She blushed. "Miss Hathaway. Mrs. Marsh, that is to say your mother, did say your skills made you slightly absentminded."

"No, of course I recall you. You're Mr. Wiggins's niece. So pleased to meet you again."

She stood with one hand on the gate, smiling at him. His heart beat faster, but only because he'd understood that she was likely the appointment Patterson had mentioned.

"You're a member of this parish?" he asked.

She hesitated. "Yes."

He couldn't allow her to go in there alone. "I was just there," he said.

"The hall? That is where I am going."

That settled it. He reached across her to open the gate for her and the maid. "But I believe I left my, um, handkerchief behind. Allow me to escort you." They walked down the winding path to the church. The flagstone path was too narrow for two, so he allowed her to go ahead, past the sanctuary toward the hall. The maid trailed behind.

Miss Hathaway held a small parasol over her head, making it difficult to hold conversation. He attempted it anyway. "Are you here about church business?"

She lowered and closed the parasol. "Yes, and I'm studying the Bible with Mr. Patterson, the curate. We are going to conduct a ladies' class, and we are organizing our notes."

He put his hand on her shoulder briefly just to stop her. Miss Hathaway jumped as if the touch was a slap. He immediately removed his hand and was glad he wore gloves so he felt nothing of her emotions or thoughts. Perhaps that annoying, irregular symptom had vanished, but until he was certain, he'd never remove his gloves.

"I beg your pardon for startling you. But I have a rather odd request to make."

Her eyes went wide. She glanced at the maid, who'd stopped near a grave and was inspecting it. He wondered if he needed to worry for Miss Hathaway, who must have this girl along for every visit. But he wasn't comfortable enough to walk away.

"Nothing unseemly, I assure you," he quickly added. He had to warn her. But he had no authority to do so. When Robert returned—he would know what to do and say. "I want a friend of mine to speak with you. That is all."

"What is it about?"

He merely shook his head. "It's best if I allow my friend, Mr. Court, to speak to you."

A large brute of a man appeared in front of them. Oliver hadn't seen where he'd come from, but perhaps he'd been lurking near the huge beech near the fellowship hall. "How do you do, sir, ma'am. Is something the matter?" The man's manner was polite, but that astonishing way he'd popped up, along with his working-class accent, would alarm any young lady, Oliver supposed.

It was no surprise Miss Hathaway moved a little closer to him. "Is this another friend of yours, Mr. Marsh?" she asked faintly.

"No, I'm afraid I have not had the pleasure. Shall we go in?" He wondered if they should simply push past the man who stood on the path.

"I heard you mention the name of Mr. Court," the man said. "You are acquainted with the gentleman?"

"You were listening to a private conversation?" Marsh was indignant—and astonished. He had not been speaking in a loud voice. This man must have been hiding nearby.

"Yes. I work with him. My name is Wilford."

All the tension drained from Oliver. He hadn't heard the name before, but of course Robert wouldn't have left without someone to watch the church—someone who had the remarkable ability to hide, despite his bulk.

He sighed with relief. "I was just advising Miss Hathaway here to, ah, keep her visit brief today. I think Mr. Court would want to speak to her. Soon. She's going to teach a Bible class with Mr. Patterson, you see."

"Just as you say, sir. I expect we'll both speak to him upon his return." The large man tipped his hat and walked away—which was for the best. What would Mr. Patterson think should he look out and see two men talking to Miss Hathaway?

She began to walk again, a little faster. "Mr. Marsh, when you speak of the Bible class, you sound as if we were plotting treason. Why are you so somber? It is all rather odd."

"I apologize," he said. "I can see I have alarmed you, Miss Hathaway."

"Not as much as that strange Mr. Wilford." She slowed and made a moue of distaste and gazed in the direction where the big man had disappeared. "But who is Mr. Court?"

"My friend, as I said. He and Mr. Wilford are also interested in Spiritualism." That wasn't a lie. After all, Robert was interested in stopping him from holding séances.

The maid still lingered near the gate and Oliver asked,

"Surely your maid will accompany you?"

She shook her head. "No, she's to go shopping and will return in an hour." Her gloved fingers clenched the Bible she held, and for a long moment she stared down at it; then she looked up at him, fear or defiance on her face. "My family does not approve of my leanings in this direction. We are Presbyterian, you see. I am more and more convinced I have a home in the Church of England."

That might explain her jumpiness.

"I shan't breathe a word to anyone." They were close to the door, so he lowered his voice and asked, "Tell me, Miss Hathaway, do you and Mr. Patterson discuss many subjects?"

"He knows the Bible better than anyone I've ever met. His scripture knowledge is astounding." She glanced at him, her brow crinkled slightly. She was a pretty young lady and fair. He noticed other resemblances to the photo Robert had of Lily. That small mouth, for example, and the trim figure.

He must allow her go in alone. Patterson surely didn't murder women every day—especially women who had maids who would wait for them. And not when the housekeeper or maid was on the premises. It would not do to have the man know they suspected him of anything.

He patted his pocket and pulled out the handkerchief. "Oh, my, I was wrong. I had it all along. I beg your pardon. Do have a good day." He gave the still-frowning Miss Hathaway a slight bow, turned and walked off.

As Miss Hathaway disappeared into the building, the maid wandered out of the churchyard. She held a basket and swung it as she strolled down the street.

"I say, miss?" Oliver walked after her.

She turned and smiled. "Oh? And what is it you say?"

He ignored her flirtatious giggle. "How often does Miss Hathaway hold private meetings with Mr. Patterson?"

"Who'd want to know then?" She cocked her head to the side.

He pulled out a pound and handed it over.

"She comes here twice a week, and maybe more often than that," she said pocketing the money. "And she's that silly if she thinks I'm hiding it. Her mum and uncle know all about her interest in this place."

He supposed a young lady would enjoy the sensation of sneaking away from authority, a small thrill in a dull life.

The maid took a step closer. "Anything else, sir? I have a free hour before I need to return."

He tipped his hat to her. "No, thank you. Enjoy your free time."

No longer smiling, she gave him the sketch of a curtsy and, swinging her basket and her hips, walked away without looking back. He waited until she vanished around the corner before returning to keep a close eye on the church from the pavement several houses away.

It shouldn't have been such a shock when the quiet voice behind him said, "You said you're working with Mr. Court? You're that Spiritualist, aren't you?"

Oliver jumped anyway. "Christ, man, you are quiet."

"Sorry, sir. It's a habit."

"It's good for your line of work, I suppose." He cleared his throat. "What did you say your name is?"

"Sergeant Wilford, sir. Did Mr. Court ask you to keep an eye on the situation?"

He didn't mention Patterson's name, of course.

"Not precisely," Oliver said.

The sergeant stood next to him. His hair was too long and his mustache untrimmed. Hardly regulation police material, though his manner was as stern as the corner bobby when he scowled. "I'm not sure what 'not precisely' means, sir. I think I must warn you to stay away from the situation until I have consulted with Mr. Court."

"Now that I know you're keeping an eye out, I agree. But I think you might need me in order to speak to Miss Hathaway."

"I beg your pardon?"

"I'm acquainted with the young lady I met at the gate, and she's not the sort to speak to strange men." He waited a heartbeat to add dramatic emphasis. He was a showman after all. "She visits Mr. Patterson at least two days a week, alone."

Mr. Wilford stroked his mustache but didn't answer right away. "Mr. Court will decide," he said at last. Oliver had to grin. It was rather comforting to know that he wasn't the only one who depended on Robert.

"Shall I wait to talk to her?"

Mr. Wilford shook his head. "No. I assume Mr. Court knows where to find you?"

"Yes. If you meet him first, then please do tell him to call upon me?"

The sergeant nodded. "Certainly, Mr. Marsh."

Oliver couldn't help trying to ruffle that stolid demeanor. "I imagine you're wondering why a subject of Mr. Court's one investigation would come barging into another."

Oliver would swear that the corners of Wilford's mouth almost tipped into a smile. "I expect Mr. Court will tell me if he chooses. Good day to you, Mr. Marsh."

Oliver had no choice and returned to his home to await Robert.

He had less than four hours to wait. And it was clear that Robert had talked to Wilford before he banged on Oliver's door.

"What the bloody hell do you think you're about, Marsh?" he said even before Oliver had managed to close the door behind him. "You approached Patterson? You spoke to some girl that visited him?"

"Good evening to you too, Robert. The answer to both questions is yes. If you'd calm down enough to listen, I shall—what would you call it? I shall give you a report."

Robert, large, rough-hewn, smelling of the outdoors and the dirt of train travel, walked into the parlor. He refused refreshment and sat on a chair, leaning forward, elbows on his knees. "Go on," he said.

Oliver repressed that urge to kiss or snarl at Robert, who was all business. Very well, he could pretend they were not lovers.

He took his seat on the sofa and related all he could remember about what he felt and saw as he shook hands with Mr. Patterson. There was an air of unreality to those moments, and trying to recall it was something like dredging up a dream hours after awakening.

"There is a hollowness in his soul that I think he must be frantic to fill," he said at last. "I haven't felt anything like it before."

"You've had this knack for only a matter of days," Robert reminded him.

Oliver frowned. He shouldn't expect a kiss or embrace from Robert, but he couldn't help wishing Robert had picked the sofa so he might sit next to him and feel that soothing pull that would allow him to relax even while his body woke in other, more interesting ways. "I think I've had a version of it all of my life. It has got too strong to ignore."

"I suppose that makes some sense." Robert rubbed the back of his neck, and Oliver wondered if he was discouraged or weary. "Now tell me about this girl. What on earth made you approach her?"

"She's a friend of my mother's. She spoke to me first, as a matter of fact."

As Oliver described the brief conversation with Miss Hathaway and then her maid, Robert gazed at him steadily, without moving or speaking. He must use that aggressively focused awareness to get information from villains. Oliver's thoughts drifted to imagining Robert wearing that predatory look and nothing else.

He smiled as he felt himself grow aroused.

"Is there any possibility he is suspicious of you?" Robert's impatient words brought him back to the present, and Oliver began to suspect that until this matter was solved, Robert was going to be a man obsessed. He was a bulldog, grabbing hold and not letting go.

Oliver described the brief encounter, adding, "I think we should call on her. I wonder if she could be persuaded to help in the matter."

Robert's heavy brow grew heavier. "No."

"Have you a better idea?"

Robert leaned back in the chair at last and stared up at the ceiling. At last he said, "No. You're right. She must be warned of the possible danger."

"Exactly," said Oliver. "And if you're going to have that sergeant lurking about the place, you might want to warn her about him, as well, so that she doesn't call the police."

Robert closed his eyes for a long minute. "If only I could run this as an official investigation. I require more resources."

"There are the three of us."

"Not enough." Robert sounded gloomy. "Tomorrow we should go speak to the young lady. You know her address? We'll call upon her at home."

"Will we go with Sergeant Wilford?"

"He will keep watch over Patterson. We'll need to speak to her guardians."

"She's of age. Why would we discuss the matter with anyone but Miss Hathaway?"

Robert sat up straighter, and Oliver could see that dangerous glint in his eye. "Mr. Marsh, this is my investigation."

He was going to let it go—one should pick one's battles, after all—but Oliver was tired. "That's not entirely accurate. You have been warned not to investigate this murder. Remember, Robert?"

"I'm a trained investigator, and I—"

Oliver interrupted. "I have been looking into the dark corners of people's lives for months now. Didn't I tell you how I find information? Even before that strange episode, I was able to read their movements, the way they sit in a chair or speak. And I have learned how to do research. I can ferret out secrets. And I am not such a dunce as to reveal what I know to Patterson. You underestimate my abilities."

Robert rose to his feet. Oliver wondered if he would storm out or insult him first. The cool gray eyes looked him up and down. "You underestimate the danger of a man like Patterson. Furthermore, you have paid no heed to anything I've told you to do."

"That's not entirely true. Didn't I lick you exactly as you instructed?"

Robert's mouth thinned, and Oliver hoped he was suppressing a smile, but no, those eyes were thunderous.

For a long minute, neither spoke, and Oliver wished he hadn't challenged Robert—and then made light of the situation. He was going to lose the first man he'd had any real interest in for years and fall back into loneliness. He wanted to back down, to apologize, but stopped himself.

He sighed and became serious again. "I don't mind taking orders from you during sex-play. I love it, to be truthful. But I am no one's minion."

"Marsh. I am not used to…" Robert stopped, rubbed his hand over his cheek. "I live alone. I often work alone or with subordinates. Perhaps I should go now. We will go tomorrow to speak to Miss Hathaway."

Oliver wanted to beg him to stay to at least indulge in a quick embrace, but he could see that Robert was troubled, and in his own tired state, they'd probably quarrel again.

"Tomorrow, then." He reached out a hand. A gentleman's handshake—surely Robert could not object to that.

Robert eyed his hand as if it held a weapon.

"Robert," Oliver said softly. "I thought of you often today." He opened his arms, and thank the Lord, Robert walked into them then and pulled him close.

"I-I can't," Robert said. He clutched Oliver so tightly he had trouble drawing breath, but he didn't feel the need to complain. He drew in Robert's scent, tightened his own arms, and it was just the two of them standing silent, in a fierce embrace rocking from foot to foot. Nothing else in the world mattered.

At last Robert drew away. He gave Oliver a wan smile. "We

will succeed," he said and didn't clarify what he meant. Would they bring down Patterson? Would they remain friends?

Oliver could only nod in answer. He found Robert's hat for him and watched his friend leave.

## Chapter Fourteen

The next morning, Court woke from only a few hours of rest, exhausted. Too many thoughts crowded his mind for sleep to come easily. Oliver had disobeyed his instructions and confronted Tom Patterson.

A jolt of fear had shot through Robert at Wilford's news, even though Oliver wouldn't have been in any real danger. He couldn't bear the thought of Oliver in the vicinity of the killer. And then foolish, infuriating Oliver had been so blasé about his disobedience.

He'd lain in bed awake most of the night, considering what he knew of Thomas Cuypers neé Patterson. Could the man have begun a pattern of wooing a young woman's trust, then eliminating her, that began all those years ago? Court and Oliver hadn't been able to learn where Cuypers went after leaving Grayfeld-on-Severn until his reemergence nearly nine years later as Thomas Patterson, newly minted Anglican cleric.

Perhaps Court possessed a touch of clairvoyance like Oliver's, for he'd always been intuitive where criminals were concerned. Now his instinct told him Cuypers/Patterson had killed before Lily and was nearly ready to kill again.

Court was relieved when daylight allowed him to leave his bed. He must warn Miss Hathaway, and the best way to do this was to have Marsh introduce them.

He dressed quickly and made his way to Marsh's rooms, where he found his friend also seemed subdued. That was a relief. Court's desperation to keep Oliver from danger was disturbing enough he didn't want to understand the implications—and he most certainly didn't wish to cope with Oliver in a challenging mood.

When they called upon Miss Hathaway, they were unlucky enough to catch her alone—and the foolish creature admitted them. Though Marsh was a family friend, she should have known better.

The girl sat on a sofa in a surprisingly large parlor, all wide eyes and innocence, while a maid sewed in a far corner—in Court's opinion too far away for propriety, but he was glad of it.

Miss Hathaway was a pale shadow of Lily, smaller, less vivid. He felt a wave of longing for his dead cousin.

"You are Mr. Court," she said before Marsh could introduce them. "And you have some information for me. Ever since I met Mr. Marsh yesterday, I have wondered and wondered what you would say about Spiritualism. Won't you please sit down, gentlemen?"

Court and Marsh sat next to each other, across from Miss Hathaway. "Please do not keep me in suspense," she said.

Court opened his mouth, intending to approach the truth carefully, but Marsh spoke immediately. In a low voice, he said, "You can keep a secret, can't you, Miss Hathaway?"

She nodded. "Of course."

"Marsh," Court warned.

Oliver ignored him. "Mr. Court is with the authorities, and we're here on a police matter."

"Mr. Marsh," Court said with more emphasis, but Oliver ignored him. He leaned closer to her and spoke quickly. "We have no solid proof, but I'm certain of this fact. Mr. Patterson is a murderer, and we are afraid he has his eye on you."

Court didn't jump up and drag Marsh from the room, but it was a near thing.

She gave a small cry—loud enough to cause the maid to put her sewing on her lap and look at them. "Miss?"

"Nothing, nothing," she said, though she'd gone pale.

When the maid seemed satisfied, Court said, "Miss Hathaway. Mr. Marsh has unnecessarily alarmed you."

"I rather think it is necessary," Oliver said. "I considered the matter long and hard, and I believe the more Miss Hathaway knows, the safer she will be."

Court considered dragging him from the room and gagging him as well, but shutting the man up was less important than dealing with Miss Hathaway, whose lips trembled.

The maid had stopped sewing and was watching them with interest.

"Is it true?" Miss Hathaway asked Mr. Court in a low voice. She had managed to calm herself, and the only sign of agitation now was the way she clenched her hands in her lap. "No, don't shake your head in denial. I can see from your grim expression it is. Tell me, what am I to do?"

This had begun as far removed from regular investigation as he'd ever ventured upon, and now he was about to involve a civilian. A young girl at that, although with each word she spoke, he was more impressed by her. "I think you must avoid his company," Court said bluntly.

"How did you come to find out about him? Why isn't he in prison? Come, sir. You must tell me." She set her shoulders and gazed at him with those eyes that, yes, really did resemble Lily's.

Reluctantly, he told her more details, including the story of Lily's death, emphasizing the fact that Lily was a clever, strong young lady. Let her understand the danger of the situation. "Yet despite our suspicions, my hands are tied. I cannot conduct an official investigation," he admitted. "Though I am not officially involved, I have looked for evidence, but, as Mr. Marsh said, there is no proof yet."

"Yet what you suspect is true. I know it is." She drew in a long breath, and her quiet words came out in a rush. "I had thought I was oversensitive. Mr. Patterson touches my hands too often. He speaks of good women of the Bible far more than any other topic. I-I had rather thought... Well, he is not bad-looking. And he seemed particularly interested, yet whenever I tried to imagine the next step..." She colored. "I mean the offer of marriage, which he has hinted at. When I thought of such things, it didn't seem as if..."

"As if he was serious?" Oliver asked.

"Oh, no, he is very serious. Mr. Patterson is *always* serious, and that is rather why I couldn't imagine the next step. He is older than I am, and that was not dismaying, not at all. But then he speaks of wives so often and with no humor. If we are right, what a dreadful man." She closed her eyes for a long minute. A tear trickled down her cheek.

"Miss?" The maid was on her feet.

Miss Hathaway waved a hand. "Please. Don't trouble yourself, Martha. I'm fine." She rose.

Court also stood, ready to ask Miss Hathaway to sit down because, now that she knew of Mr. Patterson, they had to discuss the fact that she must remain quiet and stay safe.

But she didn't dismiss them after all. "I think I need some air. Mr. Marsh, Mr. Court, would you like to see the garden? It is rather small, but the autumnal colors are pleasant."

She led them to the drawing room door, and she and Martha went through first.

Court glared at Oliver even though he was no longer sure the man had been an idiot for spilling the secret to Miss Hathaway. He simply had to glare at someone. Oliver gave him a smile. No, that was a smirk.

The gravel path through the garden was barely wide enough for two. The maid settled herself on a bench and stared dreamily into space as Miss Hathaway strolled next to Court. She quietly asked, "What can I do? How shall I help you?"

"Stay away from the man," he growled.

"How will that help you?"

"We won't need to protect you."

She shook her head. "Then he'll fix his attention on another young lady, and you'll have nothing to stop him. Allow me to help."

Behind them, Marsh gave a small triumphant sound that sounded like a cackle. Dragged away, gagged, and perhaps hung up by his thumbs, Court reflected with a sour smile.

"There is nothing you can do." Court attempted his most oppressive tone—though having to remain quiet detracted from the menace he wanted to convey. "I shall not risk an innocent's life."

She moved back, away from him, to walk next to Marsh. "You are not a policeman, but perhaps you can think of a way I might help stop Mr. Patterson."


In the end, Court had to step in with a list of rules. "You will never visit without alerting me or Mr. Wilford. You have a schedule of meetings, yes?"

She nodded.

"Good. That makes it much easier to accompany you. We

may not be in sight, but we will be close."

"Mr. Wilford." She narrowed her eyes to consider it. "The strange man in need of a haircut that we met yesterday."

Oliver, close behind them, gave a snort of a laugh, and Court had to smile, but immediately grew serious again. "I should like to talk to your mother about this. She is a widow?"

"No, no. You must not. She doesn't know I've been paying calls on Mr. Patterson, and I wouldn't disturb her for the world. She's very easily upset, you see."

"Your uncle, Mr. Wiggins?"

"Good for you for recalling his name," Oliver said. He seemed almost high-spirited now that the matter was settled. Court looked forward to having a private talk with him, although such a thing might be impossible until they'd solved the problem of Mr. Patterson. Court had already guessed that the Patterson matter would be settled soon. Pastor Wickwilly had said the attack on the village girl had happened on that night of bonfires and wild celebration. And Lily's had occurred on the same holiday.

"We must be particularly careful the closer we come to Guy Fawkes," Court said slowly. "The day may have some significance to the man."

He made Miss Hathaway repeat all of the instructions he'd given her, including the most important bit: she was never to go to Patterson alone.

"I forgot," she said and blushed. "I am to see him this very afternoon."

Court pulled out his notebook and wrote down the particulars of her appointments with Patterson. "I shall be there in three hours," he promised. "And you will be there in four. You won't see me, but I'll see you."

Miss Hathaway nodded gravely. "Thank you. And now I'm afraid you must leave. My mother will return, and she would not approve of my entertaining gentlemen when I am home alone."

"I'm afraid your mother is correct," Court said.

"Correct is not always the right path to follow." Oliver stopped next to a bush that had scarlet foliage, and leaning down to examine the leaves, he looked at Court sideways.

"Of course you'd say something like that," Court growled.

For the first time, Miss Hathaway smiled. "You are good friends, I can see that. I am greatly reassured knowing you will help."

"On the contrary, you are helping us. Thank you." Court shook her hand farewell. They bid her good-bye, and before leaving, Court made sure to slip a sizeable tip to the maid, who winked at Marsh for some reason.

Court wanted to go to a quiet place with Oliver and show him how worried he was—not to mention angry and aroused. But he had work to do.

"You're going to Patterson's church," Oliver guessed.

"Go home, Oliver."

Oliver's laugh was incredulous. "No."

Court, too tired to argue, allowed him to trail along, asking questions. And it soon occurred to him that the questions Oliver asked him helped him organize and expand his thoughts.

What if Patterson had more than one female in his sights? What evidence would Court look for in his rooms?

The plan he'd devised depended on who was in residence. If the housekeeper and vicar were absent, Court planned to search Patterson's room while Miss Hathaway kept his attention. Wilford would stay within calling distance to guard the girl.

And how the mighty inspector has slipped, he thought. Proper procedure was out the window.

"Well? What will you try to find?" Oliver prompted again.

"He might have photographs or other mementos of the other women he's...approached," Court said.

Oliver walked faster to catch up with him. Court hadn't realized he was walking so quickly. "Approached is a sweet euphemism."

Court laughed without humor. "Surely Patterson didn't murder them all. Perhaps he's saved other sorts of tokens."

"Hair. Perhaps he's even had their hair made into rings." Oliver twisted his mouth thoughtfully. The man had the most expressive mouth. "Gloves. Lily didn't have gloves that day. And Miss Hathaway mentioned he touched her hands often."

"I'd forgotten that fact about Lily." Somehow his own memory and the reminder that Oliver really had felt Lily's death made Court's stomach turn and the sense of urgency grow. "I will go speak to Wilford now."

He hailed a hansom, and they climbed in, alighting two streets away from the church.

Court pointed to a lamppost next to a small greengrocer's. "Wait here. You will not move from this spot."

"Yes, all right," Oliver said, exasperated.

Satisfied, Court left him. He walked past the vicarage and church holding a newspaper, the signal that he needed to meet with Wilford at the prearranged spot—the greengrocer's.

By the time he'd walked back to Oliver, Wilford and he were discussing the cloudy weather.

"You might as well go home," Court told him.

For once, Oliver obeyed. Court missed him almost at once.

It began to rain that afternoon, and the housekeeper was on the premises, so Court couldn't attempt the hunt through Patterson's rooms. Instead he and Wilford kept watch from the churchyard.

For two more weary days and nights, Court and Wilford and Oliver took turns watching Patterson, but he did nothing extraordinary.

On the third morning, Court at last had a chance to meet with Oliver again. They sat at a table in a pub, and for a few blessed minutes, spoke of topics other than Patterson. They had a friendly argument about the best way to train Jock to do tricks.

"He is a smart beast, Robert. You need to keep him occupied."

Robert agreed, but he wasn't about to concede. He found himself agreeing with Oliver far too often lately.

When Oliver imitated one of the men he'd met at a séance, Court laughed despite himself. He said, "I have been thinking about what you should do instead of those séances."

Oliver held up a hand. "No. If we are going to be dreary today, let us at least discuss the matter at hand. Here. I've done some research at the library."

Oliver had managed to uncover a story about a young lady in Shepherd's Bush who was found dead of suspected poisoning in her rooms. Her description sounded similar to Lily and Miss

Hathaway, although her station in life was more humble. She was a seamstress in a dress shop.

Oliver handed the notes he'd made to Court. "Do you see that she was an avid churchgoer?" He tapped the papers. "She had recently been forming a Bible-study group with several other churchgoers."

Court frowned down at the notes. Oliver's handwriting was clear and easy to read. He would have guessed it would be more florid. "The suspicion fell on her fiancé, but he was never charged. There were signs that she'd been ravished. I don't recall this case, but I've seen similar ones." He read the notes again. "There's no mention of it, but I imagine the authorities also entertained the notion of suicide."

Oliver picked up his pickled egg and popped it into his mouth. He chewed, swallowed. "She and her fiancé were to be married within two weeks. Just like Lily. And look at the date. She was discovered dead November eighth, but authorities suspect she'd died a few days earlier."

That prickling sensation hit Court, but he gloomily reflected instinct was not the proof they'd need for a trial. "I shall look for any mention of her name when I comb his rooms. It had better be soon, for we are on borrowed time, Wilford and I. Our superintendent is demanding results."

Oliver raised his hands as if in surrender. "You have them. You have driven Oliver Marsh out of business."

"Truly? What will you do instead, Oliver?"

"I have ideas." Oliver pulled his watch from his pocket. "We should get back to watching that blasted house. I must say I'm tired of that place."

"You needn't come with me. Wilford and I will be there this afternoon. I am more convinced that we need to be especially alert tomorrow." The fifth of November.

Oliver tucked away his watch. He gave Court a crooked grin. "I find I'm reluctant to leave you alone. And don't protest that I'll make a hash of keeping watch. I haven't been spotted yet."

Court smiled. "I have faith in you." And he realized he wasn't lying. Over the last few days, he'd come to understand that Oliver was capable of patience, stealth and bravery, three characteristics he hadn't suspected the man possessed. Intelligence, he knew. Sensitivity, obviously—Oliver could read people better than even Wilford, who was good. And kindness. The way Oliver reassured Miss Hathaway during their brief meetings. And humor. The way his eyes lit when he laughed...

Oh, Lord.

Court stared down at his partially eaten pasty and lost his appetite. He been silently enumerating the things he most admired about Oliver as if he was a callow young lad dreaming of his lady-love.

"Get some rest. We'll need you tomorrow," he said and left the table without another word.

As he walked away from Oliver, who hadn't protested, Court tried to think of who else he might contact for help, but knew he could depend only on Oliver and Wilford.

## Chapter Fifteen

It was a bloody awful night, wet, windy and coldly clammy. Even so, the pall of smoke hung heavy over the city, and boisterous groups of young men and some women lurched through the streets. The Guy's effigy must be burned regardless of sleet, snow, rain or fog. It was tradition. The historical significance of Guy Fawkes Day had lost importance, but the excuse for a night of drunken revelry and mayhem went on.

Oliver drummed his fingers against his thighs as he scanned the street. He felt a constant rush in his bloodstream—anxiety, fear or just plain nervous energy coursing through him. He agreed with Robert's assessment. Tom Patterson would attempt an attack on Miss Hathaway—and the three confederates, Oliver, Robert and woolly Wilford, must catch him in the act.

Oliver felt guilty and worried about the Hathaway girl putting herself at risk even with her protectors standing by. He was also irked with Robert for posting him outside of the churchyard to "keep watch". Keep watch over what exactly? Court was effectively placing Oliver out of the action, as if he didn't trust him to help apprehend the killer. Well, who had pointed the investigation in Patterson's direction in the first place, and who had uncovered information about the Shepherd girl, another possible victim? Oliver was as much a part of this case as either of the official investigators. Maybe more so, for he was the one who could feel the curate's desolate soul when he was in his presence, and he was the one who'd suffered Lily's death right along with her.

He looked over his shoulder at the looming church, the dark shadows in the graveyard with white stones thrusting like bony fingers from the earth. Somewhere among those crosses and headstones, Wilford lurked, awaiting a signal from Court, and inside the vicarage, Robert had secreted himself to watch over Carol Hathaway like some invisible guardian angel.

The woman herself had entered the gates of the churchyard nearly a quarter hour past. Oliver could picture her sitting in Patterson's parlor, open Bible on her lap as she listened to the curate expound on his theories. Miss Hathaway had allowed the curate to convince her to meet him without her maid in attendance—a liberty which only a woman who intended to indulge in licentious behavior would be likely to permit. Once again, Oliver wondered why Lily had been alone with the curate on the night she'd been murdered.

So the stage was set once again: the sacrificial lamb, Carol, swallowing her fears and daring to face a dangerous man, Court searching Patterson's room while they met, searching for more evidence to use against him but ready to burst into the parlor at any moment, and Wilford, standing by in the churchyard.

And me, out here doing nothing useful besides fretting, Oliver thought glumly.

"Penny for the Guy, guvnor?"

Oliver started as a small hand clutched his arm. He turned to see a dirty, thin-faced boy of about ten holding out an open hand.

Against his better judgment—for one street urchin could multiply into a dozen at the slightest sign of weakness—Oliver dug in his pocket and pulled out a couple of pence. He placed it on the outstretched palm. The boy tipped his cap, then scampered off into the shadows.

Oliver was struck by a sense of unreality as flickering light from barrel fires burning farther down the street sent shadows and orange light dancing wildly against the walls of buildings. The sound of singing voices and a tinny piano spilled from a pub several streets down, and from somewhere came the sound of an escalating argument. Impossible to believe that amidst all this activity, an attack might be taking place at this very minute, in the quiet order of the vicarage parlor, no less. How had Thomas Patterson or Cuypers, whoever he was, managed to lure not one but possibly numerous young women into his web to carry out his nefarious agenda? Nice young women who should've known better than to be with any man alone. Gullible young women who trusted a man of the cloth.

Pondering the whys of it was hardly useful, but Oliver had little else to do out here in the street. His gaze flicked to the spot not far away where Lily's body had been found only a year ago. He'd been able to pass by it many times now without reliving her agony, but suddenly, as he gazed at the cobblestones in the shadow of a nearby building, he began to feel a prickling sensation that was becoming all too familiar.

"Oh no. Not again," he breathed and braced himself as a wave of sensation hit him with hurricane force. A bolt of terror struck like lightning, dizziness, disorientation, the nightmarish feeling of being chased by an evil force and unable to run away. Oliver gasped for breath and clamped his fingers around the iron railing of the churchyard fence to anchor him in the world as he felt himself slipping sideways into another moment in time.

*He was stronger than I imagined. I didn't listen to you about being careful, dear. I should have listened to you. Oh, Phillip...* Lily's voice spoke directly into his ears. No. It was inside his head. He'd heard those words before, that first time at Lady

Markham's séance. But this time Oliver knew who the "he" she referred to was. With her last strangled breath, her thoughts had been of her fiancé. Feeling what she'd felt, Oliver *knew* she'd loved Phillip. His half-formed opinion that she'd been meeting the curate behind her fiancé's back evaporated.

But why, then? Why had Lily gone to the vicarage that night? Perhaps a sad tale of his need to confide in her? Anything was possible, and the truth might never be known. It hardly mattered now. It didn't change the fact that Patterson had got her alone and attempted to molest her, and she'd managed to escape into the night.

Oliver's heart raced as sensations of fear and dread mounted. *Danger, danger, danger*—the message filled his mind, pounding like a warning gong of imminent peril. The feeling was wrapped up with Lily's fear as she felt her life slipping away, but there was more to it than that.

*He will hurt others. You must help them.* Was it a direct message from Lily to him from beyond the grave or merely an echo of her final thoughts?

*This is for the best, my dear.* Oliver heard Thomas Cuypers's voice. The man was too slippery, too remorseless. How had they imagined it was safe to send innocent Miss Hathaway in to poke at that snake's nest?

Oliver shook himself, driving off the dizziness, the whispering voices and the malevolent blackness swirling around him. He must go inside *now* and make certain of Miss Hathaway's safety. Scotland Yard investigators be damned.

The gate was locked, so Oliver dashed around the side of the churchyard to a less visible spot. He climbed on top of a rubbish bin from the neighboring building and vaulted over the fence.

Court had entered the curate's cottage behind the church through a back window, an easily accomplished task since the window wasn't latched. After all, who would expect a burglar to break into the rather humble dwelling of a church's curate? If there was anything to be stolen, it would the silver collection plates or chalice in the church itself or the wealthier vicar's dwelling next door.

He'd crept through the silent kitchen and hidden himself in a small storage room at the rear of the house, where he listened to Cuypers's footsteps cross the floor upstairs. Likely the curate was in his bedroom—a place Court wanted to check for evidence as soon as Cuypers and his guest, Miss Hathaway, were ensconced in the parlor. Court felt another twinge of guilt at using the woman as bait, but he would be close at hand and Wilford only a shout away in the churchyard. Miss Hathaway was as safe as she could be under the circumstances.

Court had timed this operation, and Miss Hathaway had arrived for her assignation with Cuypers just minutes after Court had placed himself inside the house. He listened to Thomas Cuypers open the door to let the girl inside and to their footsteps and Cuypers's voice as he led her to the parlor. Likely he was inventing some excuse for there being no housekeeper to act as chaperone.

Carol Hathaway had rehearsed her reasons for coming without her maid in attendance. The stage was set for Cuypers to assume he had lured the fly into his web and to believe she was so infatuated with him, she'd thrown caution to the winds.

He would offer his guest a cup of tea. Carol would take it but only pretend to sip. She understood she must act sleepy and disoriented and that the man would likely make his move then. Court had told her to cry out the moment she felt she was compromised—though heaven knew, the young woman's reputation was compromised merely by making this unchaperoned nighttime visit.

Court let himself out of the closet and headed for the stairs to search Cuypers's room. Over the last two days, he'd managed to search every room but this one. He'd even slipped into the small parlor below when both the maid and Cuypers were out, but Cuypers had returned before Court had finished the upstairs.

Apprehending the curate for making advances on Miss Hathaway was not enough to prove his guilt as a murderer. More evidence was needed. A bottle of whatever he used to drug his victims or some memento he may have kept to recall his conquests—anything that Court could use to bring the man to justice.

He had to pass close by the parlor door before reaching the staircase, and Court paused in the shadows of the hallway to listen to the curate's droning voice. It sounded as if he were delivering dull catechism designed to lull his victim into a stupor.

"The fair sex was created as a counterpart to the dominant force which is man—the rib taken from Adam's side gave life to his weaker helpmeet, Eve. It is a woman's duty to mold herself to the will of her more intellectual, more powerful companion. So you see, you have a role to fill in this world. You needn't tax your brain with worries or fears about stepping outside of societal boundaries by coming to see me. You must trust in my good guidance."

Miss Hathaway murmured a vague agreement, and Court moved on, soft-footed, to the base of the stairs. He crept up them, keeping his weight to the far side of each step in case there were any that creaked. At the head of the stairs, he paused and listened. Cuypers's voice rolled on.

There were only two doors, and Court headed for the left one, the view from which would overlook the graveyard rather than the back wall of the church. It seemed the more likely choice for Cuypers's bedroom.

The room was dark but for a little pale light coming through the window. Court was forced to turn up the gaslight in order to explore the bureau drawers and the space beneath the bed. It didn't surprise him that his hurried search turned up nothing suspicious. Of course, the murderer would hide evidence better than that. Court checked for a hidden compartment behind or beneath any of the drawers, then moved around the room, testing the floorboards. Not one appeared to be loose.

He stopped and gazed around, feeling anxious seconds ticking past. He didn't want to leave Miss Hathaway alone with Cuypers for so long. What if something happened and she couldn't cry out?

Frustrated, he tapped on the wainscoting around the perimeter of the room, and when he noted a hollow sound, his heart leaped. He stooped to examine the wood panel and pressed here and there until he felt a slight give. The molding along the top was loose. He removed a section and then was able to slide up the panel—a cunningly hidden compartment in the wall.

Inside he found several unlabeled glass vials containing a clear liquid. He opened one and sniffed the nearly odorless contents. He would have to take the liquid to a chemist to have it identified as either a sedative or something much worse. Court slipped one of the vials into his jacket pocket. Then he examined the other contents of the hidden compartment...a small box.

Heart beating fast, he withdrew the box and removed the lid. Inside was a layer of tissue paper. He pulled back the fragile paper to reveal a kid glove, dainty, pale blue, with buttons at the wrist. A lady's glove. Only one. And beneath another layer of tissue paper, another glove. A white one with a bit of lace trim. More tissue paper and another glove, a finely crocheted black fingerless mitt.

Without taking the gloves out, Court thumbed back more layers of tissue and discovered more gloves. When he'd reached the bottom of the box, he'd counted thirteen. His stomach churned as the enormous implications of that baker's dozen of ladies' gloves washed over him. Of course, he'd had suspicions about Cuypers killing more than once, but this possible proof of thirteen lives stolen made him physically ill.

Court repacked the gloves and returned the box to its hiding place. He was inside Cuypers's house on an illegal search and though the glove collection was proof to him of Cuypers's guilt, it would carry little weight in court. What did it show except that the curate had a fixation on women's gloves? Better to take the liquid in the vial to be tested, invent some reasons to suspect Patterson, then come back with other investigators. He'd steer them toward this hiding place and let them discover its contents for maximum effect.

Now he must return to lurking near the parlor, ready to burst in and save Miss Hathaway should the need arise. He still hadn't worked out how he and Wilford could explain their presence here to their supervisor if it came to it, but that was the most minor problem when one considered they were dealing with a murderer and using a young inexperienced lady as bait.

The panel slid down into place, concealing its secret. Court fit the piece of molding back into place along the top just as Miss Hathaway's screams echoed through the house.

He cursed and pulled his weapon as he stormed down the stairs, two at a time. He rushed into the parlor to find Miss Hathaway struggling with Thomas Cuypers.

"Let her go," Court commanded, raising his pistol.

The curate whirled to face him without letting go of Miss Hathaway. He held her in such a close embrace, Court couldn't shoot without possibly hitting her. Cuypers's expression was dumfounded as he beheld the intruder in his home.

"Step away from the girl, Mr. Patterson." Court spoke slowly and distinctly.

Cuypers only clutched her closer and turned slightly so that she shielded him from Court's line of fire. "This isn't... It's not what it looks like."

"Yes, I believe it's exactly what it looks like. You're pressing your attentions on a young woman who came to you for counseling."

"No," Cuypers protested. A flicker passed over his eyes, and they widened. "You planned this. You knew. How?"

Miss Hathaway's face was contorted in terror, yet she continued to fight against Cuypers's grip on her.

Court had been a fool to imagine this precarious plan would go off without a hitch. He took a step forward. "There is no way out of this for you, Patterson. Give it up and let the woman go."

Cuypers shifted again, keeping Miss Hathaway between them and backing toward the other door which led into the parlor. "She chose to come to me. She wanted my instruction and guidance."

"Yes, I imagine." He moved another step closer.

"They always do," Cuypers muttered almost to himself. "I cannot be blamed for wanting to touch that purity." He flicked a glance over his shoulder, judging the distance to the open doorway.

Court weighed his options. He was armed, and Cuypers wasn't. A quick leap forward and he could likely subdue the curate and wrest the girl from his grip before he hurt her. But suddenly Cuypers's hand dove into his jacket pocket and reemerged with an American-made weapon, a four-shot derringer. He cocked the tiny pistol and held it to Miss Hathaway's head.

"Move another step and I shall have to kill her. I don't wish to. But look what you've driven me to. Drop your weapon."

Court recalculated. He didn't drop his weapon but slowly lowered it to his side. Now would be the time to reason with the man, and how he wished Oliver was here. He was much more likely to deftly diffuse the situation than Court was.

The sound of someone crashing through the front door, possibly splintering the frame, made all three of them jerk and turn toward the sound. Events unfolded with the speed of an onrushing locomotive: Wilford's hulking frame loomed in the doorway. Miss Hathaway whimpered and squirmed in Cuypers's arms. The curate instinctively turned his weapon toward the new threat and pulled the trigger. The derringer went off with a high-pitched bang, and Wilford jerked back as the slug hit his shoulder. Court lunged toward Cuypers intending to grab the pistol before he could cock it again.

Cuypers abruptly thrust Miss Hathaway's body at Court. She stumbled into him, knocking him backward, and he dropped his gun. Court grasped her arms and spun her aside, putting her safely behind him. He dove for his pistol on the floor, but by the time he straightened, Cuypers had ducked out of the open doorway—the one leading toward the back of the house.

Court glanced over at Wilford, who had recovered his balance and was clutching at his shoulder. "All right?"

The big man nodded. "Go after him. I'll watch over the young lady."

Court plunged through the doorway after his quarry.

Just as Oliver hurtled over the fence into the churchyard, he heard the faint sound of a woman's scream coming from the curate's cottage. His jacket snagged on one of the ornamental spikes on top of the fence, and he jerked it free before dropping down onto his hands and knees in the damp grass. His knee landed hard on a rock or perhaps a fragment of one of the crumbling headstones. Pain flared from the point of contact, and he gasped a breath through gritted teeth.

He rubbed his kneecap and hauled himself to his feet, then limped toward the buildings. Miss Hathaway's scream was soon followed by a crashing sound, which he could only imagine was Wilford breaking into the house.

Oliver shambled faster, weaving around the uneven rows of headstones and tripping over a broken-off stone half buried in grass. He cursed and dragged himself upright again. A sharp popping noise that sounded like a single firecracker going off came from the house. Gunfire? His heart pounded as he hurried toward the dark shape of the cottage. He wished he was armed, but he'd never held a weapon in his life—yet another reason Robert had placed him on lookout. With two experienced armed officers of the law on the premises, probably Oliver was superfluous. He'd likely reach the scene just in time to see Cuypers arrested.

He was nearly to the yawning maw of the wide-open front door when he saw a figure running from the back of the building. Oliver immediately knew it wasn't Court or that burly brute, Wilford, which left only one man it could be. Somehow Cuypers had escaped.

Oliver raced after him, dodging around large crosses and leaping over shorter headstones, his knee only mildly protesting. Cuypers was heading for the back of the churchyard where there was another, smaller gate. Once he got through it, he'd soon be lost in the twisting maze of city streets.

Cuypers was slowed by having to stop to unlock the gate, so Oliver was only a few yards away when the man pushed through the barrier and it clanged shut behind him. The curate cast a glance behind at the sound of running footsteps but otherwise didn't pause. For a man who lived the somewhat sedentary life as a cleric, he was fast. He ran down the alley behind the churchyard and turned the corner just as Oliver pushed through the gate.

Oliver's feet beat against the cobblestones. His foot hit a patch of something slippery, and he slid on a patch of mud or maybe decayed garbage. He caught his balance without losing momentum and dashed around the corner after Cuypers. He was damned if he'd let the man get away.

*For Lily and the other girls.* The thought spurred him on as he grew winded and his chest began to ache from the unaccustomed exercise. Oliver decided he'd been spending far too much time relaxing in drawing rooms and needed to work on keeping fit after this. As he ran, he cheered himself with the thought of wrestling Robert.

Ahead he glimpsed the cleric's white shirtsleeves. Cuypers wore no coat or jacket. The pale flash of his pumping arms as he ran made him easier to keep track of in the darkness. There were few gaslights here to illuminate the crumbling buildings or the uneven road. Although the church fronted on a quiet, industrious street, the character of the neighborhood quickly deteriorated heading in this direction.

Oliver heard the pound of footsteps behind him and cast a glance over his shoulder. Court was behind him and quickly catching up, but Oliver couldn't wait for him. He gasped for breath, pain stitching through his side, and increased his pace.

Cuypers rounded another corner, and Oliver sped after him, hurtling around the corner like a stone shot from a slingshot. Suddenly there was a throng of people blocking the way, revelers crowded around a bonfire and singing as they swayed drunkenly. Oliver lost sight of Cuypers in the press of people filling the narrow street.

Someone threw more wood on the fire, a broken chair, and the flames leaped up. In their glow, Oliver searched the crowd and caught a glimpse of Cuypers—or so he thought. He pushed past a fat man who smelled like rotten meat and snarled, "Hey, watch it!" and a woman who clutched at his arm, saying "What's yer hurry?"

"Excuse me. Pardon me," Oliver murmured as he continued to weave his way through the throng.

Ahead he saw Cuypers again, no doubts this time. He was on the far side of the boisterous crowd, dashing up a flight of stairs beside a building. Did he intend to hide in the building thinking his pursuers would keep looking for him on the street? Did he know someone there who might take him in? Or was he perhaps heading for the rooftops, a dark world of chimney pots and gables where a person could lose himself?

Oliver's legs ached as he climbed the stairs and hurried along a narrow, rickety catwalk beside the building. Cuypers was right in front of him now.

And then he was turning, spinning around to face Oliver. Oliver realized the walkway led nowhere, and the door at the end was locked, and Cuypers was as trapped as if he'd run up a blind alley. His only possible escape would be to jump off the platform to the street below. Two stories. He might just be able to do it without breaking his leg.

Cuypers pointed a hand at him, and for a moment, Oliver didn't see the tiny gun in his grip. Then the light glinted on its silver muzzle.

Oliver froze in his tracks.

"Back up," Cuypers demanded, his voice shaking, betraying his nervousness. "All the way to the stairs."

Oliver raised his hands and took a careful step backward. He wanted to play for more time, keep Cuypers distracted while Robert caught up. He prayed Robert hadn't lost sight of them in the crowd.

"Mr. Patterson, you don't have to fear me. I'm unarmed and I don't wish you any harm," he soothed. "I'm not certain exactly what happened with Miss Hathaway, but I'm sure you have reasons for whatever transpired." He stopped backing up, allowing Cuypers to approach him. A few steps physically closer gave him a chance to look into the other man's eyes. If he engaged Cuypers, he might begin to talk and lower his guard.

"You." Recognition dawned on Cuypers's face. "Who sent you to spy on me that day? Court?"

Oliver flipped through his options like stereoscopic cards he was considering slipping into a viewer and decided telling the truth might prove most beneficial. "No one sent me, Mr. Patterson. Although you might find it hard to believe, I must tell you that I felt a psychic flash the moment I shook your hand at Phillip Hasel's house." He took a deep breath and plunged on. "I know about Lily. I experienced her death during a séance and began helping her cousin, the detective, try to find out exactly what had happened to her."

He didn't say "to find out who'd killed her." There was no need to antagonize the man who held a gun on him. "When I touched your hand, I felt that vision again, but I also felt the essence of who *you* are, Mr. Patterson. I know you never meant to hurt anyone."

"No," Cuypers murmured. "That's right. I never did. It was unfortunate... An accident..."

"Because you had to hide the truth." *Over and over again.*

He thought Cuypers was going to shoot him now. But after a long silence, the man muttered, "If they would only submit willingly, I could let them live."

Oliver didn't move. He tried not to show even a hint of shock and cocked his head to the side to show he was very interested.

Cuypers spread his arms as if trying to present an argument in a debate. "But women will talk, so I had to silence them. I swear it was as painlessly as possible. The sedative in the tea is usually enough to elicit cooperation while I...get close to them, but afterward I must usher them into the next life."

"Of course you must," Oliver murmured, not yielding a step as Cuypers moved even closer. He kept his voice calm and even, a best friend, a shoulder to lean on, the trusted listener that Cuypers had probably longed for his entire life. "But somehow Lily got away from you."

Cuypers nodded. The muzzle of the gun was slightly lower, as if he'd forgotten he held it in his hand. "I never meant to choose her." In the dim light, his eyes seemed to shine, and Oliver saw he was crying. "But she was so pretty, so delicate, so...angelic. She was to marry soon and would lose that precious gift. I asked her to come to the church to counsel a wayward young woman in need of a lady's help. With her soft heart, I knew she'd follow my directive and come alone so as not to intimidate the woman. I gave her a cup of tea to drink while we waited."

Oliver nodded sympathetically while listening for the sound of Robert's footsteps on the stairs. *Hurry!* he silently urged his lover. *I can't hold his attention much longer.*

"I prayed for her that night. I know she went straight to heaven. The angel who guides me told me so," Cuypers said. He paused, then added, "God won't punish me for this. I am only trying to share God's connection with them."

"But it always ends, and then you must find another," Oliver prompted.

"Yes, that's it exactly. You understand." Cuypers was very close now, only a few steps away. If Oliver reached out, he might be able to snatch the derringer from Cuypers's hand before he pulled the trigger.

"I used to pray to my angel, the angel of stone that blessed the village. His spirit informed me I was unique and had a special mission with special privileges. I had a divine blessing, you see." He stared into Oliver's eyes. "But you're the first person I could ever tell about it."

Oliver smelled bay rum and sweat and felt the same waves of desolation he'd felt rolling off Cuypers when he'd first met him. "Life can be very lonely," he murmured.

Just then the rapid-fire pop of shots cracked through the air, *pop-pop-pop*. No, not gunfire. Firecrackers, Oliver realized. And in that same instant, he felt a sharp pain in his shoulder as if he'd been stung by a wasp.

"Oh!" he exclaimed and looked down at the neat circle in the front of his coat, the edges of the cloth smoking. He smelled the sharp tang of burnt gunpowder and glanced up to see a thin curl of smoke coming from the derringer. "Oh," he repeated.

*Now!* A voice inside screamed. Was it Lily, propelling him

into action or his own inner voice guiding him? Oliver lunged toward Cuypers before the man had a chance to cock the trigger of the derringer again. He grasped his wrist and squeezed hard, trying to make him drop the little pistol. Oliver's left arm was useless. He felt pain blooming through it, radiating out like the sun's outer rays from the burning core.

Cuypers might be insane, but he also had a strong sense of survival. And he was stronger than Oliver. He wrenched his arm away, shoved Oliver aside—luckily into the wall of the building rather than off the narrow platform onto the street below—then he cocked the pistol again.

Oliver had fallen down onto the fire escape. He stared at the muzzle, so small, but it didn't take a high-caliber bullet when the thing was aimed right at his face. He swept out his leg, knocking Cuypers's legs out from under him so the other man fell. That at least put them on equal footing.

Except the curate still had a weapon and Oliver didn't. He scrambled toward the stairs, ready to concede defeat and run for his life. It was at that moment that the sharp report of another gun tore through the air. No firecracker this time and no little derringer. This was a loud, authoritative crack like lightning splitting a tree.

Oliver looked toward Cuypers, who'd been dragging himself upright, in time to see his body jerk. Once. Twice. Three times in quick succession. Each jerk preceded by a loud report.

Oliver turned his attention toward the stairs. Court stood at the top, his silhouette black against the night sky, his shoulders broad and his coat flapping around him like...like wings. *An avenging angel*, Oliver thought, and then he lost consciousness.

# Chapter Sixteen

Court stood in front of Superintendent Hardy's desk and counted how many times the man used the words "irresponsible" and "unprofessional". Eleven for "irresponsible" and, bother, he'd lost track of the second.

He did manage to keep himself from reaching into his waistcoat to check his watch. Visiting hours at the hospital would end soon, and if he didn't get a move on, he'd miss seeing Oliver.

"Sir?"

Hardy had wound down from his rant and was waiting for a response to something he'd said. Alas, Court had been too busy wondering if he should attempt to find grapes for the visit or if he should go straight to the hospital where Oliver and Wilford lay.

"The lady's family is most forgiving, which I, frankly, do not understand. When will you call upon them?"

"I have spoken to them already, sir."

"Did I not make myself clear that Mrs. Hathaway wishes for another interview? You will attend to that as soon as possible. In the meantime, I will contemplate the future consequences of your careless, irresponsible actions..."

Twelve.

Three irresponsibles later, he was excused to return home, where he should wait for the verdict.

*The Psychic and the Sleuth*

As he passed Childs's desk, the other detective ignored him. At least he didn't wear a look of triumph at Court's disgrace. Perhaps he'd overheard the part of the diatribe during which the superintendent had grudgingly admitted that Court had found and stopped a killer they hadn't known operated in their midst.

Court had managed to keep Wilford from sharing blame; that was worth a great deal. He was fully prepared to take all blame and keep his coconspirators safe.

And thanks to a few judicious words to Lord Markham in private, the whole problem of Marsh seemed to have vanished. The newspaper printed drawings of a dramatic scene which portrayed a fine likeness of Marsh, hands up, recoiling in horror as the villainous curate fired at him. When Court had brought Oliver the papers, Marsh had laughed at the pictures and insisted on saving them. Court found them far too disturbing to examine closely.

The fact that the public opinion also regarded Court as some sort of hero was almost as disturbing. He was far more likely to agree with Hardy's assessment. Irresponsible. Unprofessional.

Opting to arrive empty-handed, he made his way to the hospital through a thick drizzle. There were only two hours allotted to visitors, and he'd already missed one.

The two men were in an open ward, but at least their beds were side by side.

Court slowed when he saw two young ladies were next to Wilford's bed. Miss Hathaway and her maid? Surely this was not the sort of place Carol Hathaway should visit, especially after her adventures earlier had already cast her reputation into doubt. But she sat placidly by Wilford's bed, reading to him as if his eyes and not his shoulder had been injured by the bullet.

Oliver's face was too pale and his eyes too bright. Please, no, Court thought with a jolt of panic. Infection could easily carry him off.

His fear dissipated—when he reached to shake hands, Oliver's fingers were cool in his. And Oliver's smile appeared genuine, without the hint of pain Court had seen on his previous visit.

Had it truly only been two days? More like a year, he thought. And at least a year of his life had been lopped off when he'd witnessed that gun pointed at Oliver.

He leaned over Oliver, pretending to adjust the other man's covers.

"She's been here since visiting hours began, and she has stopped pretending it is to see me," Oliver whispered in his ear. Ah. The bright eyes were due to suppressed amusement.

"Good afternoon, sir," Wilford called.

Court straightened, and he managed to hide his astonishment as he greeted Miss Hathaway and the sergeant. Such a misalliance. He was at least ten years older than she, and while he wasn't precisely from the streets, Wilford was more than comfortable in them. Beauty and the beast was the phrase that sprang to mind.

He certainly had no right to judge. His own version of near perfection might have melting blue eyes and lovely hair prone to curls, but he also had a sizeable cock.

"Have you granted an interview to a reporter yet?" he asked Oliver.

"No."

"The publicity would be good for your business."

"I promised you that my days as a medium were over. Did you think I lied?"

Court considered pointing out that Oliver lied for a living, but it occurred to him that Oliver hadn't lied to him for a very long time. "No, I didn't," he said, "But Lord Markham has decided that your intuitions about Patterson were proof enough that you are authentic. He has ceased badgering Superintendent Hardy—in fact he wrote him a letter suggesting the police employ your services."

"How would he know about what I saw? You!" Oliver hitched himself up. "You are the one who told the world about my intuitions." He scowled at Court. "Why would you do that?"

"Your instincts were real. They are."

"Of course they are," Miss Hathaway said. "My uncle is very impressed by you, sir," she said to Marsh. "Though he and my mother are most displeased with me."

*And me*, Court didn't point out. "If you're truly abandoning your practice, what will you do for a living?"

"I shall continue to help people with their problems." He wore that impish grin that told Court he was in a wicked mood. "I plan to set up shop to do private inquiries."

Court folded his arms. "Brave lad to be so amusing when you've got a bullet hole in you," he said.

"I'm not trying to be amusing. I'm telling the truth."

"That's absurd. It's a ridiculous plan."

Oliver's smile didn't falter. Raising his voice slightly, he said, "I told you he would respond with scorn, did I not?"

"I suspect I owe you sixpence after all," Wilford grumbled.

"You placed a wager?"

Oliver nodded. "Mr. Wilford here said you'd think it a fine plan. I knew you'd balk."

Court wanted to protest, but four pairs of interested eyes watched him for his response. The maid apparently listened as well.

He sighed. "I expect you owe me a few pennies for helping you win that bet."

"I'll deliver the moment I am released from this place." Oliver pushed at a pillow. Court leaned over him and, ignoring his protests, arranged the pillow for him.

Oliver settled back with a soft groan. "Thank you, that's better. Your aid reminds me that I shall expect help from you and Mr. Wilford as I look into what this sort of business requires. Tell me why you hate the idea so much?"

Court knew, of course. It was the image of Oliver throwing himself in front of Cuypers that haunted him. Now that he considered the work Oliver would likely encounter—finding stray husbands or runaway wives, poring through stacks of papers for the proper receipts—that was an absurd notion.

"I beg your pardon. I was wrong to protest," he said, knowing he sounded like a prig. "You should do whatever you wish, Mr. Marsh, as long as it is within the law."

Oliver wore that grin again, and Court knew the wicked devil was imagining the things he'd wish to do that would be very outside the law. This was a good sign of Oliver's recovery—and a promise for something in the future.

"To be honest, I suspect you will be good at the business."

"Thank you," Oliver said softly.

"So I was saying, sir." Wilford waved his good hand. "Got an eye for details and when a person's lying. He's got a good mind for the work, Mr. Court."

"As do you, Mr. Wilford," Miss Hathaway said.

Court suddenly wondered if the reason Mrs. Hathaway was demanding another appointment with him had more to do with discussing his sergeant than the dreadful incident two days ago.

Life was far more interesting than it had seemed an hour earlier. He'd add to the excitement.

"You want my help?" He shifted his weight from foot to foot as if he was about to jump, which he was, in a manner of speaking. Robert Court, who planned and plotted every case and almost every moment of every day, was ready to take a leap he hadn't even anticipated until this very second.

"Yes?" Oliver eyed him.

"I shall give it freely, but you must know that, because I have more experience, I will want to be in charge of most cases, particularly those involving criminal matters."

"What are you talking about, Robert?"

Oliver's incredulity brought the old, more cautious Robert back to the surface. "Well. Not right away, I suppose. I can only give you some few hours a week. But eventually, what with your gift and my doggedness, we'll make a fine go of it."

Oliver's mouth opened, but he didn't speak.

"Your agency, I mean," Robert said. "Ours, if you'd allow it."

Oliver lay back in the bed and stretched out his legs as if issuing an invitation. "Oh, yes, indeed I would allow it."

Court glanced over at Miss Hathaway and Wilford, but they were ignoring the cheeky Oliver and gazing at him, almost as dumbfounded as Oliver.

"Sir? Are you mad?" Wilford struggled on his bed as if he'd rise.

"Yes, a little. Don't injure yourself, Wilford. Lie down."

"But, sir! You're an inspector."

"And if I left, there'd be room for advancement for you. At any rate, I should leave before I am booted," he said. "I'm not sure my word will do you any good, Wilford, but I'd be glad to say something to Hardy."

Wilford was protesting again when the nurse came into the ward to announce the end of visiting hours. Court put on his hat and paused when Oliver crooked a finger to summon him close.

"They say I should be able to leave here tomorrow, but I require someone to take care of me," Oliver said. "My mother is very eager to take the job. Her housekeeper, Alice, will be tolerable, but please, I beg of you, spare me from my mother's fussing."

"You want me to act as nursemaid to you? Marsh. I'd be dreadful at it. I have no patience and would be yelling at you to get out of bed almost at once."

"Sounds perfect." He glanced over at Wilford and Miss Hathaway, who were deep in conversation and paying them no mind. "No, I'm wrong. Only one thing would be more perfect—if you'd join me there."

Court burst into laughter.


It was Mrs. Lally's day off. Hours and hours of private time stretched before Robert and Oliver without fear of the housekeeper or anyone else interrupting. One of the advantages of owning a private investigative service was that they could choose to close the office once in a while when a special occasion called for it.

Oliver had informed Robert that he'd put an explanatory sign in the office window—Closed Due to Illness—before hurrying across town to intercept Robert before he left home. "It's a beautiful day. We'll take Jock on a walk in the park, then spend a long, luxurious afternoon and evening in bed."

"Oh, we will, will we?" Robert folded his arms. "What about the Pike case or the Bosworths? There are plenty of things we should be doing."

"And we'll get to them. Tomorrow." Oliver moved in close, pressed his palms against Robert's chest and slid them up to his shoulders, leaving trails of heat in his wake. "Today is a holiday. I've declared it."

Robert grasped his arms and squeezed. "Who gave you permission to? You're an evil lad, avoiding work and trying to coerce me into joining you on your exploits. Naughty boys get punished," he growled.

Oliver's brows raised and his eyes lighted with interest. "How severely?"

"I'll show you."

Robert grasped Oliver by the back of the neck and steered him upstairs. He'd wanted to employ the rope he'd purchased for some time now, but there hadn't been opportunity for sufficient time alone. Now, thanks to Oliver, the day stretched out in decadent glory before them. He could tie up his lover at leisure and torture him until he squirmed. Robert's heart hammered with excitement, and his cock grew hard at the mental image of Oliver trussed and helpless in his bed.

He soon put action to thought, slowly peeling off the layers of Oliver's clothing so he could begin his knot-tying project. Robert was shivering with eagerness but forced himself to take his time unwrapping that lean, wiry present. Each button popped from its hole with care. Tie loosened. Waistcoat removed. Shirt. Trousers. Soon he had Oliver stripped to his drawers and was able to glide his hands all over his smooth shoulders and lightly haired chest. Robert slid his hands down Oliver's hard abdomen, where the hair grew thicker, to the waistband of his drawers. He peeled them down and beheld the object of his desire, the gold at the end of the rainbow, the treasure he could never get enough of.

Although they saw each other every day now and stole plenty of kisses and touches at the office, they didn't have an opportunity for a full, unhurried encounter like this nearly often enough to suit Robert. He would've liked to have fallen asleep beside Oliver every night and awoken to him in his bed each morning, to share meals and dog walks and casual conversation whenever they wished. But to maintain appearances, Oliver had to keep his apartment. It was difficult to spend an entire night together.

Robert brushed off the flutter of discontent for the way things had to be. What they had was certainly better than anything Robert had ever expected to enjoy. The rushed encounters he'd experienced with strangers seemed pathetic now that he knew what a deep, intimate friendship with a lover was like.

He guided Oliver toward the bed, once again with his hand lightly gripping the back of the other man's neck. Oliver smiled and gave a soft groan, bowing his head a little under that firm pressure. He climbed onto the bed and cast a glance over his shoulder at Robert. "Front or back?"

Just the submissive way he awaited direction sent a fresh surge of lust pumping through Robert. "On your back," he ordered gruffly.

Still wearing that little smirk and nothing else, Oliver stretched out on his back, hands behind his head, and gazed expectantly at Robert.

Robert went to his bureau and reached deep into the bottom drawer. Beneath winter jumpers and vests he no longer wore was the coil of white rope. Cotton. White. Smooth. He pulled out the coil and held it up so Oliver could see.

An audible gust of air escaped him. "Oh." He shifted, and his muscles flexed in anticipation.

Robert returned to the edge of the bed. He set down the bundle of rope and removed his jacket and vest. Taking his time, he rolled up his shirtsleeves, took his penknife from his pocket and unwound a length of rope. He judged how much he'd need to fasten a hand to the bedpost and cut it.

He swallowed the dryness in his throat as he moved to the head of the bed and silently held out his hand. Oliver pulled his arms from behind his head and surrendered a hand to Robert. He felt the warm muscle and hard bone and the flutter of his lover's pulse as he tied the rope around his wrist. He attached the other end of the rope to the bedpost, drawing Oliver's arm alongside his head. Then Robert admired the way that looked for a moment, the stretch of arm muscles, Oliver's fingers curled lightly to his palm, and most of all, the saucy smile as Oliver looked up at him and silently begged for more.

Robert went around to the other side of the bed and fastened that hand, then down to the foot where he lashed each ankle to a bedpost, splaying Oliver spread-eagle across the mattress. He was a beautiful sight as he flexed his muscles, testing the rope.

"Now what?" he murmured.

Robert wasn't quite certain. He'd never had a man so at his disposal, exposed, vulnerable, open—all words that added dry tinder to an already considerable blaze inside him. He wanted to attack and possess, fill Oliver's body deeply and mark him as his own with a love bite on the neck. He'd promised a punishment to his victim, so he would deliver it. But a spanking wouldn't do when Oliver lay on his back. How else could he mete out chastisement? A caning would be too severe. He didn't own a flogger or a riding crop, any of the things he'd read about in certain clandestine literature.

Oliver continued to gaze at him expectantly. So as not to lose his dominant position, Robert thought of a solution quickly. A smack from a rolled up newspaper was sufficient to deter Jock from jumping onto the furniture—when Robert bothered to try to control him. It should deliver just enough of a slap to sting Oliver's skin. Plus there was the bonus of it being a punishment commonly used on dogs, thus putting the smirking submissive in his proper place.

And there just happened to be a periodical on the nightstand. But first, Oliver should be blindfolded. The characters in the erotic stories were always blindfolded to put them at more of a disadvantage.

Robert selected one of his ties and approached Oliver, who obligingly lifted his head from the pillow so Robert could fasten the blindfold in back. "This is exciting," he said. "You won't discipline me too harshly, will you?" But his voice held not the slightest real fear. It was both gratifying and annoying that Oliver thought him incapable of truly hurting him. Maybe that was why Robert rolled the newsprint sheet extra tight and slapped it extra hard against Oliver's abdomen.

The snap resounded through the quiet room, as did Oliver's gasp. His thrusting erection twitched, and his fingers curled tighter against his palms as he pulled against the ropes binding him to the bed.

Robert lifted his homemade switch and brought it down again, this time on Oliver's chest, right across his left nipple.

"Ugh," Oliver grunted. A pink mark bloomed across his pale skin.

A little dismayed, Robert slapped the switch against his own forearm to test how much it hurt. The sting was minimal, but at the sound of the slap, Oliver jerked.

Robert smiled at his reaction. Torturing was going to be fun.

He raised the paper and slapped Oliver's cock with it, earning a sharp cry of surprise. "Oy!"

Jock came bounding into the room from wherever he'd been napping, leaping against the side of the bed and barking with excitement. He was too short to make the leap all the way onto the bed.

"Have you come to rescue me, Jock? Good boy," Oliver praised.

Robert shooed the dog out the door and closed it behind him. Without Mrs. Lally on hand, he'd assumed it would be safe to leave the bedroom door open, adding an extra fillip of excitement to the forbidden proceedings. But he hadn't counted on Jock being disturbed by the noise.

Robert observed his laughing prisoner for a moment, then stalked over to him, wrapping a hand around his throat and leaning in close. "You don't take me seriously. That is a mistake."

Oliver suppressed his laughter, although dimples still lurked in his cheeks, and he nodded. "I do take you seriously. I love having you in control, and I promise to behave."

Robert gave a little squeeze of his windpipe just to make his point, then returned to swatting Oliver with the rolled-up paper in strategic places.

With his groans and twisting and struggling against his bonds, Oliver may have been overacting a bit for Robert's benefit. But it drove Robert mad with desire and turned his cock to stone. It ached with the need to impale Oliver. The way the man was positioned, Robert could see just the shadow of his crevice and his puckered arsehole.

It wouldn't be easy to enter him unless his legs were raised higher. And then Robert realized he had the power to change that. He unfastened one of Oliver's ankles.

Oliver lifted his head off the pillow and turned his blindfolded face toward him. "What now?"

"Be quiet," Robert ordered.

He unlashed the other foot, then moved Oliver's limbs as if he were a mannequin, tying his feet to the head posts along with his hands. The position with legs and arms both raised overhead looked awkward, uncomfortable and utterly arousing. Robert tucked a pillow under Oliver's arse to lift it higher; then he stood back to admire his work.

Oliver couldn't have been more open or exposed than this. Robert could see every detail of his backside, the heavy curve of his ball sac and the lightly haired groove leading back to a clenching bunghole. His gaze zeroed in on that lovely target. Robert went to the nightstand to get the small vial of oil, but before he began lathering it on Oliver's backside, he decided to bring a flush to that pale posterior.

He applied his switch, bringing it against Oliver's flesh with a satisfying snap that made him yelp. He spanked again, paused, and again, giving Oliver time to wonder when the next blow would fall. Oliver might be jerking and whimpering, but Robert noted that his cock was leaking onto his belly. The man was definitely aroused by the spanking.

"Next time you decide we've earned a holiday, you'll check with me first," Robert said. "Understood?"

"Yes, sir. It was very bad of me. I apologize. Now fuck me, please!"

At that fervent if unrepentant plea, Robert could hold back no longer. He didn't bother to strip off his clothing. Time for a more leisurely kissing and cuddling later. Right now he wanted to ram hard. He unfastened his fly, releasing his turgid cock, and slathered it with oil.

He climbed onto the bed, applied oil down that tender crevice and into the clutching arsehole. The muscle gripped his exploring fingers, and Oliver gasped and wiggled. Prepared enough, Robert decided. He guided his cock to the entrance and pushed inside with a deep groan of relief.

He leaned forward, bracing himself against Oliver's up-flung legs and gazing down at his blindfolded face. He loved the slack lips that gasped with pleasure, but he wanted to look into his lover's eyes while he came. Robert reached down and pulled off the scarf.

Oliver blinked and looked up at him. He smiled. "There you are."

*Here I am. With you. Always with you.* Robert would never in his life say anything so romantic, but he felt it with every beat of his heart and thrust of his cock. This was about much more than passing pleasure. He was joining with Oliver, not just fucking his body. He gripped the back of Oliver's thighs and pushed into him once more.

In and out he moved, each stroke bringing him closer to that intangible peak, the little sliver of heaven on earth. Oliver's body yielded to his, wrapping around him, drawing him deep, welcoming him home in a tight embrace. The tension unfurled, the peak was achieved, and Robert began that long, delightful fall down the other side. He closed his eyes and grunted as he spent, legs shaking, cock pulsing.

When the last bit of delight was wrung from him, he opened his eyes and looked again at Oliver's devilish face with its satisfied smirk. He would wipe that smirk away with a few strokes of his hand. Robert reached between Oliver's legs to massage his cock. He pulled the thick flesh with hard tugs of his fist while Oliver groaned and fought against his restraints.

His legs must be very uncomfortable by now, maybe cramping up in their need for relief, but he was seemingly too wrapped up in pleasure to care.

He cried out—loudly—as white streams shot from his cockhead onto his belly. Outside the bedroom, Jock began to bark and scratch at the door.

Oliver recovered from his spending with a gasp that turned into laughter at the dog's increasingly frantic barking. His beautiful blue eyes opened and focused on Robert. "Who knew you were such a...stringent disciplinarian, Mr. Court."

"Clearly not my ill-behaved dog," Robert said dryly as he reached to loosen the ties that bound Oliver's ankles to the bedposts.

When Court had freed his arms as well, Oliver rubbed his wrists. "You may punish me anytime. I'll be certain to behave extra badly to earn it." He glanced toward the door. "Poor Jock. We were to take him on a walk this morning, but we've got distracted."

"Patience is a virtue, and an afternoon walk will serve him just as well."

Robert climbed off the bed and tucked his cock away. He picked up the lengths of rope and hid them deep in his drawer again. When he glanced at the bed, Oliver was still lingering there naked. So beautiful with his mussed hair, rope-burned wrists and ankles and pinkened skin.

"I've been considering something since we started the business." Oliver frowned and plucked at the coverlet.

Robert sat on the edge of the bed, nervous. Oliver sounded like he had something serious to say. "Yes?"

"It seems silly, not to mention expensive, to pay for office space *and* my apartment. Not to mention my mother's home—although I believe very soon she may become Mrs. Wiggins, and

I will no longer need to provide for her. But I wondered if I couldn't move into the office space, put a cot in the back room or some such."

He continued to pick at the bedding, and Robert understood what he was really asking. He'd considered the proposition many times himself but hadn't come to a satisfactory conclusion. He reached out and took Oliver's nervous hand.

"Oliver, I'd love nothing more than for you to move in here and share bachelor's quarters with me. Since we also share a business, it might seem a logical choice to outsiders, but it also might raise eyebrows and invite conjecture. As you know, it's a very delicate balance."

Oliver nodded and stared at their joined hands. "Which is why I suggested I maintain a room at the office for appearances."

"But you would spend most of your time here. Mrs. Lally could be counted on to be circumspect even if she had suspicions. In fact, she could probably be counted on to spread the rumor that our cohabiting was for economic reasons. This is something I've been thinking about too, you know."

He reached out to take Oliver's chin in his hand and tip his face up. "I want nothing more than to have you here morning, noon and night, but we will move cautiously. Test the waters, as it were."

Oliver's slow smile reached his eyes, and the blue shone. "You want me to live with you?"

"Do you need to ask?" Robert turned his own smile into a scowl and dropped his hand away. "Come on. Get dressed and let's go walk Jock."

"Yes, sir." Oliver saluted and bounced out of bed, cock waggling.

Robert went to let Jock into the room, and the dog raced around barking while Oliver dressed. Once Jock had heard the word "walk", even through a closed door, he went wild until his lead was fastened and he was out the door.

Oliver soon had himself put back together again and pushed a hand through his hair, settling the thick brown locks into a semblance of order. "Off we go, then."

Robert couldn't suppress a smile as he gazed at his companion. The habitual dourness, which all of Court's coworkers used to tease him about, was nowhere to be found. He couldn't rouse up a grimace if he tried, nor could he stop his foolish grinning. Oliver simply made him too damnably happy. That was the trouble. A few short months ago, he never could've imagined such a man would enter his life and seize control of it. And there was no doubt Oliver had the control. For all that he played the submissive in their sexual games, he owned Robert, heart and soul.

The old Robert Court would've been horrified at giving up so much of himself to someone, but the new one couldn't manage to feel worried or afraid. He'd placed his trust in Oliver despite the fact that the man had perpetrated fraud, deluding people into believing in him. It felt strange to allow himself such trust, but there it was. He *knew* Oliver, knew him deeply and was enchanted by the man. Possibly in love with him.

Probably.

Wasn't life an unexpected thing.

They put on their hats and overcoats, let themselves out the front door, and Robert locked it behind them. They hadn't reached the sidewalk before the elderly woman from the neighboring house hurried out from her front garden to intercept them. "Mr. Court. Mr. Marsh. I'm so happy I bumped into you. I wondered if you might help me with something."

Court glanced from Mrs. Caramel's worried eyes to Oliver's face. He'd begun to treat Oliver like a thermometer, catching a reading whenever a new client entered their office. His partner's intuition was a marvel.

A frown creased Oliver's brows. "Trouble, Mrs. Caramel?"

She looked around and lowered her voice, even though no other neighbors were in sight. "Not mine but my granddaughter's. A young man she's got herself involved with. Her parents are so worried and so am I. Could I possibly talk to you about it? I understand you run an investigative service."

Robert pulled on Jock's leash, dragging him back. The dog was frantic to be off, and honestly, so was he. This was, after all, their holiday.

But Oliver smiled and reached out to take the old woman's hand. His warm manner put people at ease, and they instinctively trusted him, while Robert was the coolly logical half of their team. "Absolutely, Mrs. Caramel. We're here to help."

Robert swallowed his disappointment and nodded agreement. "Certainly, Mrs. Caramel." Oliver was right, as he so often was, damn the man. They would always be happy to help. For that matter, they would likely be happy no matter what they did.

# About the Authors

To learn more about Bonnie Dee at http://bonniedee.com. Send an email to Bonnie Dee at bondav40@yahoo.com. Join her Yahoo! group at http://groups.yahoo.com/group/bonniedee. Her Facebook address is http://facebook.com/people/Bonnie-Dee/1352577313 or you can follow her on Twitter: http://twitter.com/Bonnie_Dee.

Summer Devon is the alter ego of Kate Rothwell who invented Summer's name in the middle of a nasty blizzard. At the time she was talking to her sister, who longed to visit some friends in Devon, England—so the name Summer Devon is all about desire. Between them, Kate and Summer have written books that have been a Romantic Times Reviewers' Choice Nominee and a three-time finalist in the Passionate Plume Award—one of her m/m collaborations with Bonnie won in 2011. You can follow her updates at www.summerdevon.com or www.katerothwell.com.

*It's all about the story...*

# Romance

# HORROR

www.samhainpublishing.com

www.samhainpublishing.com

Green for the planet.
Great for your wallet.

*It's all about the story...*

# Romance

# HORROR

www.samhainpublishing.com

CPSIA information can be obtained at www.ICGtesting.com
Printed in the USA
BVOW080833161112

305764BV00002B/1/P

## Praise for Bonnie Dee and Summer Devon's
### *The Psychic and the Sleuth*

"I highly recommend this book to all who like M/M and even if you have never read any strictly M/M before, but are willing to give it a try, this would be a great starter book. Both the authors of this book are new to me, but I am definitely putting them on my 'will read more' list."

~ *Guilty Pleasures Book Reviews*

"Robert and Oliver are the perfect example of the attraction of opposites, which heightens their need for each other. The mystery of the story is satisfying. The Victorian setting is appealing. Yet it's the romance between these two very different men, as hot and complex as it is, that makes *The Psychic and the Sleuth* such a great read."

~ *Night Owl Reviews*

"This is a great love story intertwined with mystery, suspense, intrigue, murder, ardent trysts, and two fascinating men who, together, are unstoppable. If you enjoy romantic historical fiction with lots of action and passion, you will enjoy *The Psychic and the Sleuth*. Thanks Bonnie and Summer for another delightful story."

~ *Queer Magazine Online*

FREE PUBLIC LIBRARY
OF WOODBRIDGE
**MAIN LIBRARY**
GEORGE FREDERICK PLAZA
WOODBRIDGE, NJ 07095